Books by Bruce Coville

The A.I. Gang Trilogy
Operation Sherlock
Robot Trouble
Forever Begins Tomorrow

Bruce Coville's Alien Adventures
Aliens Ate My Homework
I Left My Sneakers in Dimension X
The Search for Snout
Aliens Stole My Body

Camp Haunted Hills
How I Survived My Summer Vacation
Some of My Best Friends Are Monsters
The Dinosaur That Followed Me Home

I Was a Sixth Grade Alien
I Was a Sixth Grade Alien

Magic Shop Books
Jennifer Murdley's Toad
Jeremy Thatcher, Dragon Hatcher
The Monster's Ring
The Skull of Truth

My Teacher Books
My Teacher Is an Alien
My Teacher Fried My Brains
My Teacher Glows in the Dark
My Teacher Flunked the Planet

BRUCE COVILLE

Illustrated by Tony Sansevero

A MINSTREL® HARDCOVER
PUBLISHED BY POCKET BOOKS
New York London Toronto Sydney Tokyo Singapore

A MINSTREL HARDCOVER

 A Minstrel Book published by
POCKET BOOKS, a division of Simon & Schuster Inc.
1230 Avenue of the Americas, New York, NY 10020

Copyright © 1999 by Bruce Coville

Covelle, Bruce.
    I was a sixth grade alien / Bruce Coville : illustrated by Tony Sansevero.
        p.   cm.
    Summary: When aliens come to Earth on an interplanetary trade mission, sixth-grader Tim makes friends with the ambassador's son and together they uncover a plot to sabotage the mission.
    ISBN: 0-671-03651-3 (hc)
    [1. Extraterrestrial beings Fiction.   2. Schools Fiction.   3. Science fiction.]   I. Sansevero, Tony. ill.   II. Title.
PZ7.C8344Iaw   1999
[Fic]—dc21   99-23229
                                                                      CIP

First Minstrel Books hardcover printing August 1999

10   9   8   7   6   5   4   3   2   1

A MINSTREL BOOK and colophon are registered trademarks of Simon & Schuster Inc.

I WAS A SIXTH GRADE ALIEN is a trademark of Bruce Coville

Interior illustrations by Tony Sansevero

Printed in the U.S.A.

For Daphne and Sheri

CHAPTER
1
[TIM]

Ms. Weintraub Drops a Bombshell

I just wanted to have a friend. The part about almost getting killed and kind of saving the world happened by accident.

It's not like I didn't have *any* friends. I may be kind of nerdy, but I get along with people okay, if you don't count Jordan Lynch. But I wanted a *best* friend, someone who was my total bud, someone I could really talk to.

Linnsy Vanderhof, who lives in the apartment two floors up, used to be my best friend. We've been in the same class since kindergarten, but she doesn't like to be seen with me much these days because, socially speaking, she's much higher on the food chain than I am.

Actually, Linnsy is just plain higher than me, since she's sort of the class Amazon, taller and tougher than any of the other girls, and most of the boys, too. That's one reason I'm glad we grew up together; it makes her more tolerant of me, which means she's less likely to punch me really hard. Mostly what I get is a sock on the bicep when she thinks I've done something stupid. She calls this "a little punchie-wunchie, as a reminder not to be such a dorkie-workie." She doesn't hit me all that hard, but sometimes I worry that a few thousand punchie-wunchies—which is what I figure I'll have had by the time we're seniors—will turn my bicep into mush.

Which it sort of is anyway.

Anyway, I'm used to Linnsy. The real royal pain in my butt is Jordan Lynch, who's only been in our class for two years, ever since he got kicked out of the fancy private school where he used to go. Great system, huh? The kid is so bad they can't *pay* a school to take him, so we get him. It's too bad, because if you could pay a school to take him, I'd start a magazine drive or something to cover the costs.

Jordan sits in the back row, three desks behind me. Linnsy sits two desks over. Our teacher, Ms. Weintraub, sits at the front of the room—or would, if she were ever sitting, which she's mostly not, since she's almost always up and doing something. I really like her. She makes things interesting.

Also, she's kind of pretty.

I made the mistake of saying that to Linnsy once. (I still get to talk to her because our mothers take turns driving us to school in the morning.) She gave me a little punchie-wunchie and said, "Tim, beneath that dorky exterior beats the heart of someone from another world."

That was me. Tim Tompkins, sixth grade alien, weirdest kid in the class.

Until Pleskit.

School had only been going for a week—just long enough for me to have serious doubts about whether I was going to live through the year—when Ms. Weintraub called us together for "an important announcement."

I struggled out of the headlock Jordan had me in and started for my desk. I figured the "important announcement" was probably about lunch money or eraser duty or something, but it was a good excuse to get away from Jordan.

Once we had settled down, Ms. Weintraub said, "I'm sure you all followed the big news this summer."

3

"You mean about the aliens?" I cried.

Linnsy groaned, and I could tell by the look on her face that if I was sitting closer to her I'd be getting "a little punchie-wunchie" right then. But I couldn't help myself. Ever since the first time I saw *Close Encounters of the Third Kind* (I've watched it forty-seven times in all), I've been waiting for aliens to contact us.

So when the president announced in July that Earth had received a message from the Interplanetary Trading Federation, I had been one of the happiest kids in the world. I figured it was just about the biggest news in history. So what else could Ms. Weintraub have been thinking of?

I guess the others didn't feel the same way. At least, Jordan didn't. "Space Boy strikes again," he snickered, using one of his three favorite nicknames for me. (The other two are Nerdbutt and Dootbrain.)

"Actually, Tim is right," said Ms. Weintraub, smiling slightly. "The announcement *is* about the aliens."

"They didn't declare war, did they?" asked Melissa Farkis. She sounded like she was about to cry. But then, Melissa usually sounded like she was about to cry.

Ms. Weintraub laughed. "No, Melissa. The

aliens haven't done anything to disprove their claim that they're friendly."

I could scarcely keep myself in my seat. "So what's the announcement?"

Ms. Weintraub looked serious. "As you know, the aliens are establishing a single embassy for the whole planet, which many countries have been competing to host. The aliens have finally made their decision. They're going to settle *here*."

"Are we going to Washington to see them?" I asked eagerly.

Ms. Weintraub frowned at me. "Tim, please control yourself. And you misunderstand me. The aliens are not settling in Washington. Everyone was afraid the aliens would choose the United States, and there was some jealousy about that. So to keep it a *worldwide* mission, the aliens have decided to settle in this country—but *not* in the capital."

I tried to keep quiet, but I couldn't. "You don't mean they're going to settle here . . . as in *here?*"

I was so excited my voice squeaked on the last word.

"That's exactly what I mean, Tim. Syracuse is going to be host city for the alien embassy. But that's not all."

5

I grabbed the edge of my desk. What could possibly top this news?

"The alien ambassador, Meenom Ventrah, is bringing his son with him."

I let go of my desk and pushed on my eyeballs to keep them from bugging out of my head.

"Mr. Ventrah—I guess you'd call him 'Mr.,' though I don't know for sure—wants his son, Pleskit, to go to a public school. The government tried to talk him out of it, but he is very insistent. He says it is important for our peoples to get to know each other."

"So what public school will this alien kid be going to?" Melissa asked nervously.

Ms. Weintraub smiled. "This one. And not just this school. The announcement I wanted to make is that the world's first alien student is going to be a member of *our* class."

"Yesssss!" I cried, leaping out of my seat.

"Tim, sit down! This is not going to be easy."

"Why not?" asked Linnsy.

"Well, for one thing, it's going to focus a lot of attention on us. We'll have reporters hounding us to get in here. They'll be contacting your homes, too. Mr. Grand is having meetings with your parents today to discuss the situation. Some of you may be removed from the class."

6

"What?" I cried.

"Tim, raise your hand before speaking, or I'm going to send you out of the room."

I clamped my hands over my mouth. Getting sent out now would be horrible. (And getting pulled out permanently would probably kill me.)

"Good idea," said Ms. Weintraub, when she saw what I was doing. "Now, removals will be strictly up to your parents. Some of them might not want the media attention. Others might fear that Pleskit will carry dangerous germs."

"Eeeuw!" cried Melissa. "Could that be true?"

I waited for Ms. Weintraub to throw her out, but she didn't. She just said, "Well, if it were true, we'd be as likely to infect Pleskit as he would be to infect us. But the aliens and our own government have both certified that there is no chance of it happening."

Michael Wu raised his hand. "Won't the aliens think it's awfully rude if someone leaves the class?"

Ms. Weintraub shrugged. "I suspect they've studied us enough to know that not everyone will welcome this situation."

That's for sure, I thought, remembering the horrible things I had heard some people saying on the news.

"So when does this kid get here?" asked Jordan—*without* raising his hand, I might add.

Ms. Weintraub took a deep breath. She looked around the room, making eye contact with each one of us. Then, in a soft voice, she said, "Our new student will be joining us . . . tomorrow."

That was when I fell off my chair.

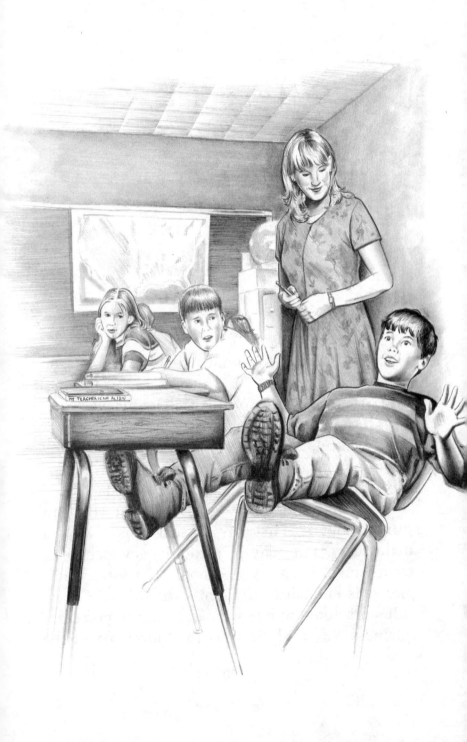

CHAPTER
2
[PLESKIT]

A Letter Home
(Translation)

FROM: Pleskit Meenom, newly arrived on Planet Earth
TO: Maktel Geebrit, on Planet Hevi-Hevi

Dear Maktel:

How are you doing? Better than me, I hope. I miss Hevi-Hevi already! And I'm scared.

I wouldn't admit that to anyone but you. But think about it. First day of school is always a little scary. First day in a totally new school is even worse. First day of school on a totally new *planet* is enough to frighten a *flinkel!*

It's not like I'm a newbie at this interplanetary business. After all, Earth is the fourth planet the

Fatherly One has dragged me to. Well, fifth, if you count that three-week disaster on Geembol Seven—*which I don't!*

Anyway, it's not like I haven't been around. But this time is way different, for one simple reason: We are the *first* off-world embassy to open on this planet! Can you believe it? These people have never met *anyone* from another world!

Well, that's probably not entirely true. I'm sure there were explorations and secret landings and so on before we decided to make formal contact. And I've found rumors on GalactaNet that some misfits have used the planet as a hiding place in the past. But that has all been in secret. I will be the first kid from another world ever to be here in the open.

I feel like I'm going to the zoo. Except all the animals will be looking at *me*.

Fortunately, I had training modules to get me ready for this, so I have a working knowledge of the language. Actually, I should say *a* language, since they have hundreds of them! (Can you believe it? The confusion must be astonishing.)

I am trying to learn enough of their customs to be able to appear in public without embarrassing myself. According to the modules, Earthlings have a strange insistence on pure truth, so *that*

11

is going to be a little tricky. But as the Fatherly One always says, "When in Gimplikt, do as the Gimpliktians do."

I wouldn't worry about all this so much, except for one more terrible thing: the Fatherly One has insisted I go to a *public* school. On a civilized planet that wouldn't make so much difference. But according to the Fatherly One's secretary,

Mikta-makta-mookta, being different is a big problem here. From what she tells me, everyone on this planet likes to pretend he or she is unique and different. (How unique and different they can be when they only have two sexes is something I cannot understand. Can you believe it??? Well, as I told you, this is a very weird place.)

Mikta-makta-mookta also says that even though they like to *pretend* they're all unique and different, at the same time each of them is desperately trying to be just like everyone else.

I don't have any idea what they're going to do when they have to deal with someone who's *really* different.

I had a long conversation with the Grandfatherly One about all this last night. He keeps telling me not to worry, everything will be fine.

That's easy for him to say. He's dead!

Thank goodness I still have him with me. Also my pet Veeblax. It is almost two years old now, and has mastered many new shapes since the last time you saw it, Maktel, though it still hasn't found its name. If the Fatherly One had not allowed me to bring it along, I doubt I would have been able to stand this trip. Sometimes I almost think it understands the things I say to it. I wish I had a talking pet, like you do. But that will have to wait until we're much wealthier than we are now.

Anyway, I told the Veeblax how I felt about being sent to such a primitive place. I can't complain too much to the Fatherly One, since one of the reasons we got this nasty assignment is because of the problems back on Geembol Seven.

The good side to all this is that if we can manage to find something on Earth that will interest the Interplanetary Trading Federation, the Fatherly One will have a lifelong interest in the planet's commerce. Of course, that means we're going to have to sample virtually every food that exists here, trying to find something truly special. My stomach aches just thinking about it! But aside from new foods, there's not much a primitive place like this could offer the rest of the galaxy.

So that's my father's goal. I have three goals:

1) Find a friend. (I know you won't take that personally, since we both agreed long ago that whenever we go to other planets we have to make new friends.)

2) Do not embarrass the Fatherly One by destroying this mission the way I did the last one.

3) Find some excuse to come home to Hevi-Hevi.

I'm sorry this is such a depressing transmission. But you made me promise to write and tell you about my trip, and a promise is *meetumlicht*.

So I'll keep sending these messages.

I hope you enjoy them. I have a feeling it's going to be a lot easier for you to read about all this than it will be for me to live through it.

Tomorrow morning I leave for my first day at the new school. I should be sleeping, but I can't. I'm too scared!

I will write and let you know how it goes.

Until then—*Fremmix Bleeblom!*

Your pal,
Pleskit

CHAPTER
3
[TIM]

The Changes Begin

I knew he was going to start with one of those letters to Hevi-Hevi. Okay, here are a few pages from my journal:

Holy Moses! We got the coolest news today. We're going to have an alien kid in our classroom! This is the best thing that has ever happened to me. Ever. *EVER!*

I can't wait to meet this new kid. I figure after all the science fiction I've read, I'll be the person in class most ready to be friends with him.

I'm amazed at how fast this is all happening. Ms. Weintraub says it's because that's how the aliens work, and everyone is trying to keep them happy.

I was wondering where the aliens were going to stay. I got my answer when I was walking home: They'll be living in Thorncraft Park. The reason I know this is because there is a big hill in the park, which I can see as I cross the bridge on the way home. I can also see it from my bedroom window, which was always nice, but is now *very* cool, because this is where the embassy is going to be.

Now here's the really weird part: The embassy is there already! That is too strange. This morning there was no building on the hill. Now there is!

Actually, *on* is the wrong word, since the embassy doesn't actually touch the ground. It hangs from a curve of silvery-looking metal. Even though the footing of the curve is a couple of hundred feet long, it's only a few feet thick. Looking at it, you can't imagine it could hold anything up.

But it does. It arcs about two hundred feet into the air and bends over in a kind of a stem.

And hanging from that stem is . . . a flying saucer! Well, it's not actually flying. But I bet it could.

It looks like this:

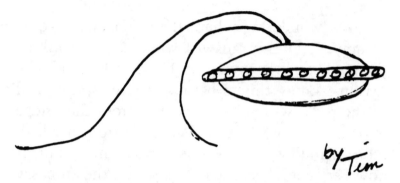

I HAVE TO GET INSIDE IT SOMEHOW!

Other developments:

1. Ms. Weintraub told us that tonight the school will be installing a Personal Needs Chamber for the alien kid.

"What's a Personal Needs Chamber?" asked Chris Mellblom.

Ms. Weintraub smiled. "We would probably call it a bathroom."

"This kid gets his own bathroom?" cried Jordan. "That stinks!"

"How do you know, Jordan?" asked Michael Wu. "You haven't smelled it yet!"

The alien's bathroom is going to be in the old art storage room, the one I used to hide in when Jordan was bugging me too much that first year he came to our school.

2. A couple of government guys pulled Mom out of work for the parents' meeting yesterday. She told me that when her boss objected, they flashed their badges and he stopped squawking immediately.

She claims that when the Feds first came in, she was afraid I had gotten in some kind of big trouble. (Thanks, Mom!) She is a little scared about the alien himself, but she says the government guys convinced her there's no chance of me picking up a weird alien disease or anything.

I asked her if any parents were going to pull their kids out of class.

She said she didn't know for sure, but that a couple of parents were pretty upset. (Mrs. McLory didn't believe the government people about it being safe, and Mr. Gardell wanted to know what religion the aliens were.) Mom said that Jordan's dad acted real weird, too, but she figured that was just because he was trying to figure out how he could make money out of the situation.

Well, Mom just yelled for me to go to bed. I don't know what the point is. I won't sleep a wink tonight.

Tomorrow I get to meet my first alien!

CHAPTER
4
[PLESKIT]

My Bodyguard

When I walked into our new kitchen the morning of my first day of school I found a tall, dark-skinned Earthling leaning against the counter. He was dressed in a black suit.

"What are you doing here?" I asked, feeling frightened.

"You must be Pleskit," he replied. "My name's McNally. Robert McNally. I'm going to be your bodyguard."

"My what?"

"Your protector."

I was very puzzled by this. "What are you going to protect me against, Mr. McNally?"

He moved his shoulders up and down, a gesture

I later learned is called a shrug. "Cuckoos. Crazies. Bad guys. Anyone who might want to hurt you."

My fear deepened into terror. Until now, my worries about school had all been social ones: Would the kids like me? Would I do anything to embarrass the Fatherly One? Would I experience emotional damage? It had never occurred to me I would be in *physical* danger.

"Why would the kids want to hurt me?" I asked. My *clinkus* was so tight I could hardly get the words out of my mouth.

Mr. McNally made a tiny snorting sound. "Not the kids. Well, probably not. Mostly adults. Outsiders."

"But why?" I asked again.

He did another one of those shrug things. "Because you're different. That's all it takes for some folks. You scare them."

This was such a horrifying thing to say that it convinced me the training modules were right about Earthlings telling the absolute truth. Why would he say such a thing unless he absolutely had to?

The Fatherly One's secretary, Mikta-makta-mookta, came scurrying into the kitchen. Though it is hard to read her expressions with all that fur on her face, she seemed a little embarrassed. "I'm so sorry, Pleskit! I had intended to be here to introduce you to Mr. McNally."

"Please," he said. "Call me McNally. Just McNally."

"As you wish," said Mikta-makta-mookta. But her attention was all on me. Her voice dripping with disapproval, she said, "I thought we had discussed what you were going to wear today."

I groaned. "Do I have to?"

She wiggled her nose, a sure sign she was annoyed. "Of course you don't *have* to, Pleskit. I'm sure it won't bother your Fatherly One in the least if you ignore his wishes in this matter. Why would you want to bother to present yourself well to your new classmates anyway? No, you can go as you are."

My *sphen-gnut-ksher* was starting to spark. Without intending to, I reverted to speaking in Hevi-Hevian. *"Gezup-gezop!"* I said, popping the knuckle on my left thumb three times.

At once, I realized that I had broken the Fatherly One's order about using only Earth language so we will get comfortable with it. "I'm sorry," I said meekly.

Then I went to change my clothes.

*   *   *

The question "What should I wear to school?" gets more complicated when you move to a new planet.

When I had discussed the matter with Mikta-makta-mookta the night before, she had said that for the first day I should go in a *kling-ghat*, which is what we wear for formal occasions on Hevi-Hevi.

(That's the best way I can figure out to write *"kling-ghat,"* by the way; the full name for it involves two hand gestures, a large burp, and a tiny fart. But those don't translate into Earth languages very well.)

I would have preferred the simple clothes I had been wearing, which were not unlike what Earthlings call a shirt and pants. But I did not want to disappoint the Fatherly One. So I went back to my room and put on my *kling-ghat*.

"Much better," said Mikta-makta-mookta when I returned to the kitchen.

I sat down at the table and ate some *febril gnurxis*, my favorite breakfast food. Based on what I have sampled of Earth foods, I'd say it's a little like brown sugar and ice cream, with some crunchy bits mixed in. It's very nutritious.

Shhh-foop, whom you Earthlings would call

the cook but we speak of as "the queen of the kitchen," came sliding in. (Shhh-foop's full name is "Shhh-foop <click> [onion smell], but there is no good way to do that in Earth language.)

"Would you like a cup of coffee, Mr. McNally?" she sang.

"Thank you, Shhh-foop," said McNally. I could

tell he was trying hard to keep his voice normal and not to stare. I did not take this as a good sign. If Earthlings thought Shhh-foop, who is only a 3, looks strange, how will they react when they meet someone at the far end of the Physical Chart—someone who is a 20, or a 40?

Shhh-foop slid across the floor to a clear glass counter and slapped it with one of her tentacles. A small door popped open and a steaming pot of black liquid rose as if from nowhere. Next to it were several cups. Shhh-foop filled one, then carried it back to McNally.

He took a sip. A strange expression crossed his face and I could tell he was trying hard not to spit the liquid out.

"Oh, dear," sang Shhh-foop, using her voice of tragedy. "I fear I have not yet learned the proper way to brew this Earth beverage. I will work on it while you are gone today."

"Thanks," squeaked McNally. He put down the cup. "Come on, Pleskit. Let's go."

I swallowed hard, made the small fart of nervousness, and followed him out the door.

CHAPTER
5
[TIM]

Trouble

Mom was driving me and Linnsy to school the next morning when I saw the first signs of trouble.

"Uh-oh," I said. "Look at that!"

"I couldn't miss it if I tried," muttered my mother.

The sidewalks on both sides of the street ahead were thronged with people. The only thing keeping the mob from filling the street itself were police barricades.

The police had also set up a roadblock at the next corner, where they were stopping every car that approached. Most they motioned to turn away; a few they let go forward.

On the north side of the street stood a cluster of grumpy-looking people carrying handmade signs painted with sayings such as **ALIENS GO HOME** and **KEEP OUR SCHOOLS ALIEN FREE!** and **EARTH IS FOR EARTHLINGS!**

Across the street another group was holding similar signs—except these all said things like **WELCOME ALIENS!** and **THE ROAD TO THE STARS HAS OPENED!** and **THE FUTURE IS HERE AT LAST!** These people were cheering and waving, and if not for the fact that I was actually going to *meet* an alien that morning, I would have asked Mom to let me get out and join them.

"Look!" said Linnsy. "There's Senator Hargis!"

I groaned. Senator Helm Hargis was not only the leader of the anti-alien forces, he was also one of the loudest and most obnoxious people in the world. He was holding a bullhorn (an appropriate term in this case) and ranting about how the aliens were going to mean the end of life as we know it, and besides, if God had wanted us to have aliens on Earth, he would have put them here to begin with.

"How can he get away with saying stuff like that?" I asked.

Mom shrugged. "It's one of the trade-offs for

27

having free speech: Any idiot can say whatever comes into his head."

Photographers' flashes were going off everywhere. Guys with videocameras were trying to fight their way over the barricades.

I wondered, a little nervously, what the aliens would think of all this fuss.

When we got to the police barricade Mom took out the ID card the government guys had made for her. She had showed it to me the night before. Using alien technology, it had her genetic code imprinted on it.

The cop slipped the card into a black box. The box began to beep softly. The cop handed back the card and waved us on.

Things were a little quieter once we got on school property—mostly because the cops had put a barricade all around the building.

"That wouldn't really hold if people decided to rush it," I said nervously.

"I don't think you need to worry about that," said Mom. "They're not angry or anything. Well, a few are. But most of them are just curious."

"I am, too," I said. "We've seen pictures of some of the aliens, but since there are thousands and thousands of planets in the league, we don't know what *our* alien will look like!"

"I'm sure you'll be nice to him, no matter how he looks," said Mom as she pulled over to the curb.

"Of course he will," said Linnsy. "Tim's a real sweetie pie." She said it so nicely Mom didn't even notice she was making fun of me.

We climbed out of the car. As Mom was pulling away, I heard a roar from the crowd. Turning, we saw four motorcycles pulling into the school driveway.

Behind the motorcycles came an enormous black limousine.

The crowd surged forward.

"Get back!" cried the cops, struggling to hold people in place. "Get back!"

It did no good; the waiting crowd broke through the lines. In less than an instant the limo disappeared beneath the mob.

"Wait!" I cried, starting forward. "Don't—"

A pair of strong arms grabbed me from behind. "That's no place for you, Tim. Get inside. *Now!*"

It was Mr. Grand, the principal.

I struggled to get free. "We've got to help!" I cried.

"The police will handle it," said Mr. Grand, carrying me toward the door. "What do you think you could do about it, anyway?"

I stopped struggling. "Nothing, I guess."

Mr. Grand put me down once we were inside the school. "Don't worry, Tim. Those idiots weren't hostile, just curious. And that limo could survive a small explosion. Now get on down to your room. I'll bring Pleskit in once things have settled down."

"Geez," said Linnsy as we started down the hall. "This is even weirder than I expected."

Most of the kids were already in the room, some of them looking pale and nervous.

"What a mob!" said Rafaella Martinez as Linnsy sat down behind her. "Did you have any trouble getting through it?"

"Eyes front!" shouted Ms. Weintraub, flicking the lights on and off. "Let's get started." She had to flick the lights three times before we all got quiet.

"Well, this is clearly going to be an exciting morning," she said, once we were settled. "I just got a note from Mr. Grand. It will be a little while before our new student gets here."

"If he gets here at all," I muttered nervously.

"In the meantime, let me update you on where things stand with us. I'm sorry to tell you that three students have been switched to other classes."

Everyone began looking around. "Who's gone?" asked Melissa. (Truthfully, I was surprised to see that *she* was still with us.)

"Marcus, Danielle, and Bobby," replied Ms. Weintraub. "I'm going to miss them very much, but there was nothing we could do about it. Now, when Pleskit gets here, I want you to treat him like any other student. Let's make him feel welcome but not overwhelmed. It's all right to be curious, but remember, you'll have a whole year to get to know him."

"Yeah, Tim!" hooted Jordan. "Don't hit him with all your Space Boy questions in the first ten minutes."

"Keep a lid on it, Jordan," said Ms. Weintraub sharply. "Now, one more thing—"

She was interrupted by Mr. Grand's voice coming over the loudspeaker. "Ms. Weintraub?"

"Yes, Mr. Grand?"

"Pleskit is in the building. I'm going to give him a brief tour before I bring him to your room."

"We'll be waiting!" said Ms. Weintraub.

If I haven't exploded by that time, I thought.

To keep us busy, Ms. Weintraub told us to take out a piece of paper and start listing questions

31

we had for Pleskit. "We won't be asking them all today. But over the next few weeks we'll give him a chance to share some information with us about where he's from, while we do the same for him."

I took out some paper. But even though my mind was throbbing with questions, I couldn't concentrate enough to get even one of them written down. I looked at the clock.

8:45.

I turned my attention back to the paper, trying to force myself to write something. But all I could think about was how cool it would be if the alien and I could be best friends.

I waited until it felt like half an hour had gone by before I looked up again.

8:46.

I wonder if your head can actually explode from excitement? I thought.

The minutes crawled by, moving slower than a one-legged tortoise climbing uphill through a molasses spill.

Finally someone knocked at the door. I leaped to my feet. I was finally going to see the alien!

CHAPTER
6
[PLESKIT]

Tricky McNally

We rode to school in a long black vehicle, driven by a man named Ralph. Ralph did not talk. He just drove.

"Some limo, huh, kid?" asked my bodyguard as he held open the door for me.

"It smells bad, Just McNally," I replied, speaking truthfully.

He looked at me strangely. "What did you call me?"

"Just McNally," I replied. "Isn't that how you said you like to be named?"

He sighed. "When I said 'just McNally' I meant just 'McNally.' Not 'Mr.' McNally. Just 'McNally.' Get it?"

"No."

He sighed. "Call me McNally. Don't add any-thing in front of it. Okay?"

"You got it, McNally," I said, relieved I had finally figured out what he meant.

"Good. Now let's get moving."

The limousine (I learned later that that is the full name for this kind of vehicle) actually rolled along the ground! This was a strange, and not very pleasant, sensation. And it actually *burned* a liquid called gasoline (which was what I had smelled). I understand that this is standard for Earthling vehi-cles, but for me it was quite shocking.

We had gone only a little way when four mo-torcycles pulled in front of us.

"Escorts," said McNally.

"They're so loud!" I cried, covering my ears. (They were smelly, too, but I didn't bother to mention that.)

McNally said nothing. But I saw him roll his eyes.

My discomfort turned to fear when we got near the school and I saw hundreds of people, many of them shouting and holding up signs.

"What is that?" I cried.

"Your welcoming committee," said McNally. "Come on, we're going to make a transfer."

Our vehicle stopped. McNally opened the door and slipped out, ducking down so that his head did not show above the door. He gestured to me to join him. We went to the back of the limousine. Waiting behind it was a much smaller car, light blue, covered with dents.

"Get in the backseat," said McNally.

I did as he asked.

The motorcycles and the limousine started forward. "Look," said McNally. He was pointing to a small screen mounted in the front of the car. It showed the limousine. As it drew near the school a group of Earthlings burst forward. They swarmed over the big black car like *gnucks* that have spotted a wounded *skakka!*

McNally laughed. "Morons," he said. "Come on, kid. We're going in the back way."

I decided I liked McNally. He was tricky. And as the Fatherly One always says, "Tricky is good."

McNally I liked. The rest of the planet I wasn't so sure about. The sight of those people swarming over the limousine had terrified me.

What if I had still been inside it?

*   *   *

35

We were met at the rear of the school by a tall man with long gray hair tied together at the back of his head. (I learned later that this is called a ponytail. Then I found out that a pony is a four-legged animal that people ride. Language here is exceedingly strange.)

"Greetings, Pleskit," said the man, holding out his hand. "I'm Mr. Grand, the principal. Glad to have you with us. Hope you didn't have too much trouble getting here."

"Piece of cake," said McNally.

"That would be nice," I said.

"What?" asked McNally.

"A piece of cake. That sounds good."

McNally laughed. "You don't understand," he said.

Well, that was certainly true. And what I really didn't understand was *how much* I didn't understand. That only became clear as the day went on.

"You look a little nervous," said Mr. Grand. "Let's go to my office for a little while before I take you to your room."

"Have I been bad already?" I asked nervously.

Mr. Grand looked startled. "What makes you think that?"

"My training modules taught me that bad children are sent to the office of the principal."

Mr. Grand laughed. "Well, that does happen. But good kids get to see me as well. We can skip the office for now. I'll give you a tour of the building."

As we walked through the halls, children clustered at the doors of their rooms, crying, "There he is! There he is!"

"They're anxious to meet you," said Mr. Grand. "If you're willing, we'll have an assembly next week so you can say hello to everyone. Ah, here's the special bathroom they installed for you last night."

"Bathroom?" I asked. "Do I have to bathe before I can enter the classroom?"

"Your Personal Needs Chamber," said McNally.

"Oh!" I said. I felt better. Life is always easier when you know where you're going to *finussher.*

"And this is your classroom," said Mr. Grand, when we had gone just a little bit farther.

I felt a wave of nervousness. I was about to meet the people I was going to spend the next year with. After what had happened outside, I wondered what they were going to be like.

Mr. Grand knocked on the door.

We heard a shout from inside, followed by a terrible bang.

I let out a shriek of terror and clutched my middle.

CHAPTER
7
[TIM]

Social Disaster

Talk about wanting to die of embarrassment! When I jumped to my feet, I sent my desk crashing to the floor. It landed with a sound like a gunshot. The class burst into laughter. I blushed so hard my cheeks felt like they were on fire. So much for my plan to be really cool the first time I met the alien.

The door swung open. I saw Mr. Grand, looking really cranky. To his right stood a tall black dude wearing a dark suit and sunglasses. And between them? Between them was my dream come true: an honest-to-goodness alien!

He looked totally terrified.

"Who made that noise?" snapped Mr. Grand.

"It was Tim!" yelled Jordan.

40

I WAS A SIXTH GRADE ALIEN

Mr. Grand gave me one of his looks. "Will you settle down, Tompkins? You nearly scared our new student to death!"

"I feared someone was trying to assassinate me," said the alien, his voice quivering.

A couple of the kids started to laugh, then stopped when they saw that he wasn't joking.

I wanted to crawl under my desk and hide—only I couldn't, of course, since I had just knocked it over.

"Sorry," I muttered.

I was so upset that it took a few seconds before I could really focus on the alien. He could easily have passed for human, except for three things:

1. He was totally purple.

2. He was totally bald.

3. He had a single stalk growing out of the top of his head. The stalk was about five inches long and thick as a pencil. From its top sprouted a walnut-size knob.

He was wearing a long-sleeved white robe decorated with strange designs around the cuffs and the bottom edge. It took another few seconds for me to realize the designs were shifting and changing, almost as if they were telling a story.

"Jeez," muttered Jordan. "He's wearing a *dress!*"

"Shhhh!" I hissed as I tried to wrestle my desk back to a standing position.

Jordan rolled his eyes.

Ms. Weintraub rushed over to the alien. "Greetings, Pleskit! We are so happy to have you in our room."

The purple boy smiled, then held out both hands and made some rapid motions with his fingers. An astonishing variety of cracks and pops came from his knuckles. After that, he burped. Loudly. The knob at the top of his head began to glow, and I caught a faint odor that reminded me of raspberry jam.

Some of the kids began to laugh.

"That is the traditional greeting on Hevi-Hevi," said Pleskit. "I thought you would like to see/hear/smell it."

"It was cool!" I said, still struggling with my desk. "Do it again!"

Pleskit looked puzzled. "That would be silly."

I felt as if I had been slapped.

"Where is my seat, please?" asked Pleskit.

"Right this way," said Ms. Weintraub quickly. She escorted Pleskit to an empty desk two rows over from me.

The tall man who had been standing behind Pleskit entered the room at the same time. He strolled to the back corner farthest from the door and leaned against the wall.

Ms. Weintraub turned a questioning look toward Mr. Grand.

"This is Robert McNally," said the principal, gesturing to the tall man. "Pleskit's bodyguard."

The man nodded to the class. "You can call me McNally," he said. "Just McNally."

"Do you have a gun?" asked Jordan eagerly.

McNally smiled and spread his hands, but said nothing.

Jordan rolled his eyes again. "Just a rent-a-cop," he muttered under his breath.

Pleskit leaped to his feet. "That is an unseemly comment!" The knob at the top of his head began to glow. A smell like mustard and onions wafted across the classroom.

"Whooie!" cried Jordan, waving his hand in front of his face. "Who farted?"

"I am expressing an opinion," said Pleskit.

Ms. Weintraub clapped her hands. "That's enough! I want you all to take your seats. Later, I hope Pleskit will answer some questions about his homeworld, as I know we are all very curious to learn about it. I'm equally sure that he has many questions about our world." She turned to the principal and said, "I think we'll be fine, Mr. Grand."

Mr. Grand, obviously relieved to be told he was not needed, said, "Just call if you need me, Ms.

Weintraub." He left quickly, closing the door
tight behind him.

McNally leaned back in the corner.

Pleskit sat back down. The knob at the top of
his head had started to droop. A smell like dying
daisies drifted across the room.

"Are you all right, Pleskit?" asked Ms. Weintraub.

"I am feeling a bit *klimpled,*" he said softly.
His voice was soft, and he sounded scared.

I wanted to rush over and pat his shoulder. I
would have said, "Don't worry, Pleskit. I'll be
your friend! I'll help you with all this." But I
knew Ms. Weintraub wouldn't have appreciated
it. And Jordan would have made fun of me for
the next six months. So I just sat there, feeling
as helpless as a fish in a sandbox.

"Don't worry," said Ms. Weintraub cheerfully.
"You'll be fine."

"It's not me that I am worried about," said
Pleskit sincerely.

"What do you mean?" asked Ms. Weintraub.

"Just what I said. I am not worried about me.
It is Earth for which I have great fear!"

"I knew it," moaned Melissa. "The aliens *are*
going to destroy us!"

"Why would we do that?" asked Pleskit. "We

have nothing against Earth. My fear is that you will blow *yourselves* up before we can establish a decent trading relationship. Really, you are such primitive and aggressive beings that it is an amazement you have survived this long."

I groaned and put my face down on my desk, listening to the angry murmur that rippled through the classroom. Linnsy was always telling me that, socially speaking, I was a hopeless idiot. But compared to this kid I was a genius.

"Surely you must have some good things to say about the planet," suggested Ms. Weintraub. She was smiling, but I could hear a hint of desperation in her voice.

"Good things?" said Pleskit. "Not that I can think of. No, wait! There is one thing. I do admire your commitment to absolute honesty. Other than that, I think this is a miserable excuse for a planet, and I desperately wish—"

"Good grief!" cried McNally. "Look at the time! Sorry to cut this short, Ms. Weintraub, but Pleskit has to be somewhere in twenty minutes. Official business you know. Sorry."

Then he grabbed Pleskit and hustled him out of the room.

CHAPTER
8
[PLESKIT]

The Fatherly One

"Where do we have to be?" I asked McNally as we hurried down the hall.

"Anywhere but here," he muttered.

That was when I understood that I had messed up again. My insides felt the coldness of *pizumpta*.

"You all right?" asked McNally. "You don't look so good."

"I'm not sure. I feel like I'm about to go into *kleptra*."

McNally looked worried. "What the heck is *kleptra*?"

I searched my brain, then said, "I can find no matching word in English. The closest thing the

46

training module gave me is something about pos-
sums. But that doesn't make any sense."

"Can you hold on long enough to get out of here?"

"I believe so."

We stopped at the office. "Anything wrong, Mr.
McNally?" asked Mr. Grand.

"Nah, we're fine. But I have to get Pleskit here off
to another appointment. We'll see you tomorrow."

"That wasn't exactly true, was it?" I asked as
we left the building.

"Close enough for government work," muttered McNally.

If I had not been so upset, I might have asked
him what he meant. I wish I had. It might have
saved a lot of trouble.

Ralph the Driver was waiting with the limousine in front of the school. The crowd was mostly
gone, so we drove away with no problem. The
only ones left were a few protestors, still carrying
signs saying they wanted me to go home.

I felt exactly the same way.

When we entered the embassy—which, for the
time being, *was* home, but didn't really feel like
it yet—we went to the kitchen. Shhh-foop was
sliding around the floor, singing to herself. *"Erna*

bernna blimblag, leezle skeezig!" she crooned
when she saw me.

According to McNally, Shhh-foop looks something like a six-foot-tall stalk of orange celery
with an octopus growing on its head. It took me
a while to figure out why he seemed to think
this was strange. I keep forgetting how little
Earthlings have seen of the world outside.

I sniffed the air. "You've been busy!"

"Busy?" sang Shhh-foop. "Oh, *busy!* Yes, happily
busy, cooking for Mr. Pleskit. Here, try one of these."

She opened the heat machine with one of her
tentacles, then reached in with another and
pulled out a glowing blue ring. *"Peezle gleezit,"*
she warbled proudly. Turning to McNally, she
added, "Would you like one, too, Just McNally?"

"No thanks, Shhh-foop."

"I've been working on my coffee," she sang.
"Would you like to try some of that?"

McNally sighed. "Sure, I'll try it."

"Coming right up!"

"Thanks," he said when she placed the cup in
front of him a moment later.

Shhh-foop watched anxiously as McNally took
a sip.

His face twisted in a horrible expression.
"That's not quite it," he gasped.

"Oh, pity, oh, woe," sang Shhh-foop, so mournfully I almost wept. "Ah, well. Better luck next time, eh, Just McNally?"

Once I was safe in my room, I invited the Veeblax to play on my desk. It scampered about, changing itself into various shapes, which made me laugh. After a while I pulled out my download box. This is a black cube, slightly smaller than my head. I placed it on my desk, then adjusted a dial on the side. Leaning forward, I inserted my *sphen-gnut-ksher* into the box. When it was in place, I pushed the Start button.

The box hummed and grew warm. Memories of the day's events began to pour from the *sphen-gnut-ksher* into the box's holding tank. When the memories had been downloaded back to the beginning of the day, the box beeped twice.

I inserted the box into the playback device, then put on my view goggles to watch everything that had happened. I used speed play on the less important parts. But the parts where things had gone wrong I played over and over.

"I don't understand," I muttered to myself. "I spoke pure truth, just as the training modules suggested. Yet the more truth I spoke, the more upset my classmates became. What could I have been doing wrong?"

I decided to speak to the Fatherly One.

To get to the Fatherly One, I first had to get past his secretary. She was sitting at her green desk, stuffing her furry cheeks with mook-pods when I entered the room. When she saw me, she pushed the pods to the backs of her cheeks, which bulged out to make her face almost twice its usual size.

"Greetings, Pleskit," she said. Despite her full cheeks, her words were perfectly clear. I noticed that she was getting comfortable with the new language faster than any of us.

"Greetings, Mikta-makta-mookta," I replied, bending my *sphen-gnut-ksher* toward her in a sign of respect. "Is the Fatherly One available?"

"He's with Barvgis. But perhaps he will see you anyway. Let me check."

She touched a button on her desk.

A light flashed in response.

"He's available," she said.

The door to his office swung open.

I had to look up to speak to the Fatherly One, since he was sitting in his command pod, which raises him about five feet above the floor. The deeply padded chair has a clear blue shell curving around and over it, leaving a two-foot wide opening in the front. Both armrests hold keypads where he can enter commands and queries. On the wall facing the command pod was a large screen covered with numbers and figures. Before I could read them, the Fatherly One pressed a button. The numbers rippled and a landscape from Hevi-Hevi took their place. The purple sky, the waving trees with their drooping branches covered by thick pads of orange fur, the roving herd of *pinglies*—it all gave me a painful surge of homesickness.

Barvgis, the Fatherly One's slimeball assistant, was standing in front of the command pod. (I understand from Tim that *slimeball* has a bad meaning to Earthlings, but in this case it is just a description. Barvgis is basically round and basically slimy.)

"Greetings, Pleskit," he said when he saw me. "How did your first day go?"

"Not well."

"So I have heard," said the Fatherly One. "Principal Grand called to speak to me. Barvgis, will you give us a brief time alone?"

"Certainly, Elevated One," said Barvgis. He farted respectfully and left the room.

Despite the Fatherly One's welcoming tone, I couldn't help but notice he was keeping one eye on a screen in the lower corner of his command pod.

"I fear I have disgraced us again," I said. My *sphen-gnut-ksher* was drooping in shame.

"I am sure you will do better tomorrow," said the Fatherly One. His voice was more gentle than I had expected.

"How can I do better tomorrow, when I do not know what I did wrong today? I spoke the absolute truth, just as—"

Before I could finish, a light began to flash in the command pod. The Fatherly One raised his hand and cracked several knuckles in front of the light. Then, when he realized I was standing there, he remembered his own order about speaking the native language, and repeated his words in English. "What is it?"

"I need to speak to you right away!" said Mikta-makta-mookta urgently. "It has to do with Senator Hargis."

The Fatherly One sighed. "I apologize, Beloved Childling, but I must deal with this."

"Of course," I said. "I don't mind."

This was a lie, of course. But the rule about telling the absolute truth only applied to my dealings with Earthlings.

CHAPTER
9
[TIM]

Zap!

"So what do you think?" said Linnsy as we were driving to school the next morning. "Should we start a petition to see if we can get the alien kid sent back to where he came from?"

"Linnsy Vanderhof!" cried her mother. "Shame on you!"

"You should meet this kid, Mom," protested Linnsy. "He's the most stuck-up brat I ever saw."

Mrs. Vanderhof glanced over her shoulder, to where I was slumped in the backseat. "And what do you think of that, Mr. Timothy?" (She always called me "Mr. Timothy.")

"Well, he did kind of offend people yesterday, Mrs.

V. But I'm hoping it was just because he was nervous."

"There, Linnsy," said Mrs. Vanderhof as she swerved to get back on the road. "Why don't you try to be as open-minded about this as your friend?"

I sighed. Linnsy was sure to give me a punchie-wunchie for *that* before the day was over.

The classroom was very subdued that morning. Pleskit was wearing another robe, a lot like the first one, only light green. McNally took his place in back, so quiet and unmoving you might have thought he was someone's project or something.

I was hoping we'd have another question-and-answer session, but I guess Ms. Weintraub wasn't taking any chances on Pleskit making himself more disliked than he already was.

We worked quietly through the morning, making our way through reading and spelling with no real problems. No one was outright rude to Pleskit; mostly they just pretended he wasn't there. I couldn't tell how he was taking it. I mean, even if he *had* been frowning or smiling, which he wasn't, how could you be sure what that meant on an alien face?

I noticed that he went to his Personal Needs

Chamber fairly often. It was sort of weird, since his bodyguard always went out with him.

I was still dying to get a chance to talk to the alien, of course. But we were sitting two rows away from each other, so I didn't have much of a chance. The one time I thought I could manage it, he got up to go to the bathroom again. I couldn't wait for recess. I figured that's when I would make my move.

The clock was doing its usual trick of getting slower and slower the closer we got to lunchtime. I got approximately no work done, since my brain was totally focused on figuring out what I was going to say to Pleskit when I caught up with him on the playground. This is something I had been thinking about for years— what should be the first words I would say to an alien if I ever met one. I had finally settled on, "Let there be peace between our planets."

I couldn't wait to say it.

Lunch starts at 11:40. At 11:39 Mr. Grand opened the door. Standing behind him were two people: a very pretty woman with red hair, and a muscular Asian guy carrying a big video camera marked CNN.

"We need to see Pleskit for a little while," said Mr. Grand.

I sighed. It looked like I *still* wouldn't be able to talk to Pleskit. I wondered if I would ever make contact with him.

"Our own little TV star," muttered Jordan as Pleskit and McNally left the room.

I knew the tone in his voice. It was not a good sign.

We were on the playground when McNally and Pleskit came out of the building. The reporter and the video camera guy were still with them.

McNally said something to Pleskit, who listened carefully, then started walking toward a group of kids standing near the swing set. Figuring this was my chance, I started in Pleskit's direction.

I noticed the reporter asking McNally a question.

I had almost made it to Pleskit when Jordan appeared as if from nowhere and elbowed me aside. "Out of the way, Nerdbutt. I wanna have a little talk with the purple kid."

He had his friend Brad Kent with him, which was another bad sign. Jordan liked to show off for Brad.

"Jordan!" I said. "I was here first."

"Forget it, Dootbrain," he said, giving me another shove. Then he yelled, "Hey, Plastic! You have a good time talking to the reporter?"

Except for the stupid nickname, the words were perfectly fine. It was only his tone of voice that was insulting, and that just barely. That was Jordan's way. He started slow, and sometimes you didn't even realize he'd been making fun of you until he'd gotten in two or three really good digs. But once he had you hooked, he could really do a mental slice and dice.

Pleskit turned to Jordan. "It was acceptable."

I noticed a lot of other kids moving in, the way they do when something is going to happen.

"Acceptable?" asked Jordan, sounding fake-surprised. "Well, I suppose you're used to it. You a big star back on Planet Purple?"

Pleskit looked puzzled, and a little uncomfortable. "My home is called Hevi-Hevi."

"And is everyone there a fatty-fatty?" asked Jordan. This earned him a cackle from Brad.

The knob on Pleskit's head was starting to twitch. "Obesity is not a problem among our people," he said. He spoke calmly, but it sounded like it was an effort.

"You calling Earthlings fat?" asked Jordan, stepping closer to Pleskit. He was about six inches taller than Pleskit, if you didn't count the knob.

Pleskit looked really distressed now, as if he simply couldn't understand what was happening. I wanted to step in and stop Jordan, but didn't know how. Heck, I couldn't even protect myself from the creep.

"You hear me, Purplebutt?" asked Jordan, reaching out to give Pleskit a little shove. "I asked you a question."

I looked around for McNally. He was still tangled up with the reporter.

"Don't touch me," said Pleskit.

Jordan gave him another shove.

"I'm serious!" said Pleskit. "Don't touch me!"

The knob on his head was really fizzing now. I was relieved to see McNally running in our direction. The cameraman was right behind him. Before they could reach us, Jordan gave Pleskit another shove.

The knob on Pleskit's head made a sizzling sound. A bolt of purple energy came blasting out.

Jordan let out a squawk and fell over backward.

Pleskit groaned and fell to his knees.

Jordan lay on the ground without moving.

CHAPTER
10
[PLESKIT]

Disgrace

I did not mean to blast Jordan like that. But as we say on Hevi-Hevi, "Sometimes the body has a mind of its own."

It did not help that my actual mind was not working all that well at the time. The stress of our move to Earth, the disaster of my first day at school, my fear of screwing up—all these things had weakened my resolve. So when Jordan became more and more threatening, I lost control of the *sphen-gnut-ksher*. It moved into protective mode and sent out an energy surge.

Even so, I did not expect it to be such a problem. I mean, I had not injured him or anything. But as soon as I heard people start to scream,

I knew I had been wrong about that. I was in trouble again.

These people must not understand kling-kphut *very well,* I thought. Then my knees bent and I fell to the ground.

As I dropped into Recovery Mode, I heard Ms. Weintraub scream, "Pleskit, what have you done?" This made me sad. I liked Ms. Weintraub and did not want her to think badly of me.

Roaring for everyone to stand aside, McNally elbowed his way through the crowd. He knelt beside me, but I could tell he was confused. Should he tend to me or—since I was clearly still alive—go see to Jordan? But Ms. Weintraub was already with Jordan. So my bodyguard knelt beside me and said softly, "You all right, kid?"

"I will recover." I shook my head slightly. "A blast such as that pulls a great deal of energy out of me. As soon as my *sphen-gnut-ksher* gathers more, I will be fine."

"Yeah, yeah," he muttered. He was looking around protectively. "Look, I can understand why you might want to blast that Jordan twerp. But you'd better tell me quick how bad it is. What did you do to him?"

"I put him in *kling-kphut*," I said.

Looking beyond McNally, I saw we were surrounded by kids. But instead of crowding in, they were standing several feet back. They looked excited—and frightened.

Mr. Grand pushed his way through the group, roaring, "Get back! Get back from here, all of you!" He stopped in front of me. Staring down, he screamed, "Look, Pleskit, I don't care what planet you're from, you can't bring a weapon to school!"

I felt my *clinkus* shrivel up. No one had ever spoken to me like this before. *Ever.* Not even on Geembol Seven.

I put my hand to my head, clutching my *sphen-gnut-ksher* protectively. "This isn't a weapon," I said. "We don't believe in weapons. It's part of my body!"

I was shaking, and my nose was shedding copious tears.

"Look!" cried one of the kids. "He's got purple snot!"

"It's not snot!" I replied. "It's tears. I weep for your people."

Suddenly I heard a familiar voice. It was Kitty James, the television woman I had been talking with earlier. She no longer sounded friendly. Her voice harsh, she asked, "What do you have to say for yourself now, Pleskit Meenom?"

I looked up.

She was holding a microphone toward me.

Trang, the man with the camera, was standing behind her.

McNally leaped to his feet. "Get that camera away from here!" They began to wrestle.

Terror and embarrassment flooded through me. Despite my solemn vow that this time, for once, I would not mess things up, disgrace again seemed waiting to devour me. All I could think was: *My father will be furious.*

"He's not breathing!" shouted one of the people who was kneeling over Jordan. "He's not breathing!"

"Of course he's not breathing," I said, disgusted at their stupidity. "I put him into *klingkphut!*"

McNally pulled away from the cameraman. Kneeling beside me again, he fixed his eyes on mine. His voice intense, almost pleading, he whispered, "Pleskit, tell me straight out. Is that kid going to die?"

The question was so absurd that I began to laugh.

McNally drew back, looking shocked and horrified.

That stopped my laughter cold. "Of course he's

not going to die," I said. "In fact, when he wakes up—which will be in about ten minutes—he's going to feel quite a bit better than I do right now."

Kitty James didn't show that part on television.

She just showed me laughing when McNally asked if Jordan was going to die.

CHAPTER
11
[TIM]

Begging

After Pleskit zapped Jordan, they closed school for the day. This was complicated, since most of our parents work, and the school had to call and make sure we all had places to go.

Personally, I thought they should just have kept us there. Jordan was up and walking, so it was clear he was all right. So why make such a big deal out of it? Sometimes I think people only get upset because you tell them they're supposed to. It's like my cousin Jared, who's learning to walk. When he falls down, he doesn't cry—unless his mother happens to notice him and goes running over yelping, "Jared! Are you all right, sweetie?" Then he busts into tears and cries like crazy.

But no one asked my opinion, so we got sent home. Linnsy and I walked together. The fact that she was willing to be seen with me shows she was pretty upset. "Do you think it's safe to be around that kid?" she asked me three times.

"Of course it's safe, Linnsy. He's more afraid of us than we are of him!"

But I wasn't sure she believed me.

We stopped at the top of the bridge, which gave us a really good view of the embassy rising from its hill in Thorncraft Park. I thought it was the most beautiful thing I had ever seen.

"Maybe Pleskit will have a birthday party, and we'll all get invited," I said hopefully.

"What makes you think he was born?" asked Linnsy.

I was impressed. That was a very good question.

When I got home, Mom was there, watching TV. CNN was playing the footage of Pleskit zapping Jordan. I would have thought it was a coincidence, me walking in at that very moment, but as it turned out they were playing that scene every five minutes. I bet anyone who spent an hour watching TV that afternoon could have closed their eyes and run the footage in their head, they would have seen it so many times.

Then they showed Pleskit laughing when McNally asked if Jordan was going to die.

It made him look horrible, like a monster.

"That's a lie!" I cried, the first time I saw it.

"The film doesn't lie, Tim," said my mother wearily.

"Well, it's not telling the whole truth. I was there. I saw it. The reason Pleskit laughed was that the very idea that he had killed Jordan was stupid. He hadn't even *hurt* him, for pity's sake. He just put him to sleep for a while because he thought Jordan was attacking him. Which he was. They don't show him talking about that. So they're lying!"

My mother started to say something, but the next thing they showed was an interview with Senator Hargis, and we both wanted to hear it.

It was disgusting.

"I repeatedly warned the president that this kind of thing could happen," said Senator Hargis. "No good can come of letting these so-called extraterrestrials take root on American soil! What more evidence do we need that these aliens are hostile, that they should not be allowed to walk among us? What kind of fools are we, to let them

BRUCE COVILLE

into our world without a whimper of protest? The time has come to send them back to where they came from!"

"He makes me sick," I said.

"I don't like him much, either," said my mother. "But I'm beginning to wonder if he might have a point."

"Mom!"

"Listen, Tim—I'm not sure what's going to happen. But if they let that boy back into school, I want you to stay away from him. I'm just not convinced it's safe to be around him."

I couldn't believe my ears. My own mother was turning into an anti-alien bigot.

The time had come for the Ultra Beg, which is a tactic I only take out under extreme circumstances. Throwing myself on the floor, I grabbed her feet and began to plead.

"Please, Mom, oh please please please please please. You don't know how much this means to me. It's the most important thing in my entire life I have been waiting forever to meet an alien I want this more than anything else in the entire world and if you don't let me be friends with him I'll probably die and even if I don't it will ruin my life and I'll never be the same again and probably grow up to be some warped psychotic or

68

even a criminal mastermind or something and it will be all your fault because you thwarted my deepest desire and I want this more than anything else I've ever wanted ever ever ever so *PLEASE* don't tell me I can't be friends with him!"

For a while I thought I had her. The Ultra Beg always gets her laughing (you have to hear it yourself to get the full effect, since I do really good pleading sounds). But despite the fact that she got laughing so hard she couldn't breathe, when she finally calmed down and wiped the tears out of her eyes, she said, "Oh, Tim. I know how much you want to be friends with Pleskit. But I don't want to get a message from school some afternoon telling me that my son has just been fried. No. Stay away from him."

I felt totally betrayed. I figure if you get someone to laugh like that, they really owe you a favor. Besides, Mom was just plain wrong on this one. Then, to make things worse, she hit me with the one thing I can't answer and can't joke about.

"Listen, Tim. You're my only guy now that your father's gone. I can't stand the thought of losing you, too."

We were at the edge of a major fight. It was

sidetracked by Linnsy, who had come down to fill us in on the latest news. (Linnsy's Mom is like gossip central; if there's any dirt to be had, she's got it.)

"Not only is Jordan fine," said Linnsy, "he's bragging about being the first victim of alien aggression. His father has announced he's going to file a lawsuit against the aliens, and against the government for letting them settle here."

"They got the ingredients for Jordan and his father from the same pot of puke," I said, sticking my fingers down my throat and making gagging noises.

"Tim!" said my mother.

"Well, it's true. You've got to let me try to be friends with Pleskit, Mom. Don't you see what's at stake? The aliens can take us to the stars. They can save us from ourselves!"

"Or they can just fly away and leave us to rot in our own pollution, and blow ourselves up," said Linnsy.

I looked at her gratefully.

"Sorry, Tim. I still want you to stay away from him."

I had never disobeyed my mother before, at least, not in anything big. But we had to prove to the aliens that we were worthy of their friendship. *I* had to prove it, since I was sure I was the only one who could really understand Pleskit.

I was going to make friends with him even if it killed me.

Which, as it turned out, it nearly did.

CHAPTER
12
[PLESKIT]

Gloom and Doom

For the second day in a row I got to go home early. The difference was, this time everyone else went home, too.

McNally barely spoke as the limousine drove us back to the embassy. At first I thought he was mad at me. But just before we got there, he muttered, "Sorry, Pleskit. This wouldn't have happened if I had been watching more closely."

The idea of having someone to blame was very tempting. But I sent him the smell of sorrow and said aloud, "It is not your fault."

"It happened while I was your bodyguard," said McNally gruffly. "That makes it my fault."

* * *

The news had reached the embassy ahead of us, of course. Mikta-makta-mookta met us at the entrance. Her beady eyes, usually so bright, were dulled by concern.

"Things are not good," she said.

"Does the Fatherly One want to see me?"

"He will, when things settle down a little. Right now he is talking to the president of our host country. The secretary general of the United Nations is waiting on another line. And he has to contact Perffl Giffikt at Galactic Headquarters."

I groaned. Perffl Giffikt, the Fatherly One's boss, is not very tolerant of mistakes—especially ones made by me.

"Come," said Mikta-makta-mookta, taking my hand. "Let's go to the room where food is made."

The rest of the staff was there already. You could feel the gloom in the air. Even Shhh-foop was unhappy. Her tentacles were drooping, and she barely cared when McNally choked on his coffee and then set the cup aside.

"Your Fatherly One should have listened to the advice he was given," grumbled Barvgis. He was eating fresh squirmers, which he always did when he was upset.

"What advice?" I asked.

Barvgis bit the head off a squirmer and sighed.

"The High Council did not want you to come on this mission. But Meenom refused to consider leaving you behind. 'If I go, I take my boy with me,' he said, over and over again."

This gave me very confused feelings in my *plinktum*. I was surprised, and happy, to learn that the Fatherly One had insisted on bringing me. But it also made me feel worse than ever that I had let him down.

"What can I do?" I groaned.

"Nothing, probably," said Barvgis gloomily. He picked up a whole handful of squirmers and stuffed them in his mouth, ignoring their tiny screams. "Looks like we're about to get recalled from another planet," he said, tucking in one of the squirmers that was trying to crawl out. "Maybe I should start packing."

If I hadn't already known how bad things were, that would have convinced me. It was almost a relief when the Bloop-Bloop sounded, summoning me to the Fatherly One's office.

The Fatherly One was pacing back and forth in front of the command pod. As soon as he saw me, he waved his hands, cracking his knuckles in a symphony of distress. His *sphen-gnut-ksher* was emitting the odors of despair.

After a moment he stopped. Changing to Earthling talk, he said, "I apologize for breaking my own rule about not using our native language. But today's events have driven me to vexation!" Then he farted angrily. That made me nervous; it was unusual for him to swear like that.

"Do you have any idea how difficult you have made things for me—for us—for the mission?" he asked.

"Is it really bad?" I replied, my voice meek.

"Is a *plonkus* fat? I have been working since we first made contact with the Earthlings to convince them that we are not dangerous. It has taken you less than two days to create an image that undercuts everything I have done— an image being broadcast repeatedly all over the planet."

"But I did not hurt the boy!" I said desperately. "I only put him in *kling-kphut!*"

"What really happened does not matter!" said the Fatherly One. "This is politics. What matters is what people *think* happened. Have you seen the news coverage?"

He burped a command and the large screen lit up. The face of Kitty James, the woman who had

75

interviewed me, appeared. She looked very serious. At first I thought the Fatherly One had contacted her on his communicator. Then I realized that he was showing me her broadcast.

Speaking in tones of deep concern, she said, "After the alien blasted young Jordan Lynch, he showed a depraved indifference to the effects of his action."

The screen cut to a picture of me lying on the ground, with McNally leaning over me. "Pleskit," he whispered, "tell me straight out. Is that kid going to die?"

The me on the screen began to laugh. McNally drew back, looking shocked and horrified.

I waited for the screen to show what I had said next—that Jordan wasn't going to die, and in fact he would feel better than I did when he woke up. To my horror, the segment ended with me laughing at McNally's question.

"That's not fair!" I cried. "It doesn't show everything that happened!"

"Fair is not the issue," said the Fatherly One. "When you are on display, as we are, you have to be twice as good as everyone else." He sat down on one of the lumps in the floor and put his head between his hands. "Perhaps I asked too

77

much of you, putting you out in public like that."

"No, Fatherly One," I said, sinking down beside him. "It is I who have failed you. I feel great sorrow."

He put his arm around me, which he does not do very often.

"Is it true that we may get recalled?" I asked.

He emitted the smell of uncertainty. "That possibility exists. Perffl Giffikt is not happy."

"Perffl Giffikt is never happy," I pointed out.

The Fatherly One smiled just a little bit at that, then said, "Well, he is *very* not happy right now."

I wanted to ask what it would mean if we were to be called back, but I was afraid to. I thought the answer might be too upsetting to bear. Then I remembered something else that was bothering me. "There is one thing I do not understand," I said. "If Earthlings value truth so much—"

My question was interrupted by the voice of Mikta-makta-mookta coming through the speaker. "I have managed to contact Senator Hargis. Do you want to speak to him now?"

The Fatherly One groaned. "I must take this call, Son of My Heart. We will talk more later."

As I left the room of the Fatherly One I wondered two things:

1. How could I possibly undo the horrible mess I had created?

and

2. Why was he talking to Senator Hargis?

CHAPTER
13
[TIM]

My Great Plan

After dinner Linnsy came down to give us her mother's gossip update. When my mother went to the kitchen to make some popcorn, I leaned over and whispered, "I've got to talk to you."

"So talk," said Linnsy, not bothering to whisper back.

"Privately! Let's go to my room."

"You've got to be kidding!"

"What's wrong with going to my room?"

"Well, for one thing, your mother will fuss."

That was true. The last time Linnsy and I had gone to my room for a private conference Mom had said, "You know, you kids won't be able to do that much longer."

It had taken me a minute to realize what she was talking about. When I *did* figure it out, I was totally disgusted. "Mom!" I cried. Later, I tried to explain to her that (a) I was about as interested in trying to kiss Linnsy as I was in having my toenails removed by a madman with a pair of red-hot pliers and (b) even if I *was* interested in Linnsy—which I am not, *not*, NOT—she is about as likely to want me for a boyfriend as Barbie is to date Barney. We may be friends from way back, but when it comes to the wider social world, Linnsy and I are from different planets.

"Mom will fuss, but she's not ready to go on the warpath about it yet. What's the second problem?"

"I forgot my Lysol and my rubber gloves."

Linnsy is of the opinion that my room is somewhat unsanitary.

"I'll give you some newspaper to sit on," I said. "This will only take a minute."

She sighed and followed me to my room. I had been wrong about it taking only a minute; it took about five minutes for me to find a spot for her to sit, even with the newspapers (which I had been joking about but which she insisted on).

"Tim, this place is worse than the county landfill," she said while I was scrambling to clear a spot for her.

"Are you nuts? The stuff there is all garbage. The stuff here is priceless."

"Yeah, I'm sure your ancient Tarbox Moon Warriors action figures are going to fetch a big price on the collector's market. So what do you want to talk about anyway?"

"Pleskit. I've got to make friends with him before he thinks we all hate him."

"So? I'd like to make friends with him myself."

"But *I* understand aliens," I said desperately. "Heck, I just about am one!"

"That's true. But what does it have to do with me?"

"I've got a plan."

"Tim, the last time you had a plan, I ended up grounded for a week."

"That was two years ago!"

"Right. Because two years ago I was dumb enough to get involved in that idiotic papier-mâché scheme of yours. Since then I've known better."

"Just listen to this one," I pleaded. "You won't have to do much. I'll be the one taking all the risk."

She sighed. "I know I'm going to regret this. But go ahead. Tell me what it is."

"I want to get into Pleskit's private bathroom."

"What?"

"I can't see any other way I'll get a chance to talk to him. People are always interrupting, or dragging him away."

"But it's *totally* off limits. Besides, it's locked."

"Yeah, but I've got a key."

"You do not."

"Do too!"

She narrowed her eyes. "How did you get it?"

"Remember two years ago, when Jordan first came to our class and he used to bug me so much?"

"He still does."

"Yeah, but I can cope with it better now. Anyway, Mrs. Smathers used to let me go down and work in the art storage room, just so I could get away from him."

Linnsy's eyes widened. "And you never gave back the key?"

I shrugged. "I meant to. But she left at the end of that year, and I never quite got around to it—"

"There's a lot you 'never quite get around to.' Okay, so you've got a key. I still don't know what you need me for."

"Two things. First, you can help me *find* the key."

She looked round my room and burst into laughter. "It's your barnyard, Tim—you dig through the manure!"

"Okay," I said, trying to keep from losing my temper. "I'll find it on my own. But when I do, I'll need your help to create a distraction so I can get out of the classroom."

"What kind of a distraction?"

"Well, you could faint or something."

"You'd better have a talk with your mother. Something in your breakfast cereal seems to be affecting your mind."

"Linnsy!"

"Tim, if you think I'm going to make myself look like an idiot in front of the whole class just so you can sneak into an alien bathroom, you're even goofier than you look."

"Linnsy, I've got to—"

"Forget it!"

I sighed and followed her out of the room.

Mom gave us a look, but didn't say anything until Linnsy had gone.

After Mom's lecture I started looking for the key. I turned up a ton of cool stuff that I hadn't seen in a long time, which kind of slowed me down, because I kept getting distracted by it. But no key. Then Mom started telling me to go to bed. After the third time I had yelled, "Just a minute, Mom!" she came to my door and said fiercely, *"Now, Buster."*

So I sighed and went to bed—which slowed me down even more, because it meant I had to pretend to be asleep for about an hour before I could start looking again.

It was about midnight when I finally found the key.

It was taped to the underside of my desk drawer.

I had put it there so I would know where it was if I ever needed it again.

CHAPTER
14
[PLESKIT]

Guys in Suits

"This may be my last day with you," said Robert McNally as we got into the limousine to go to school on Thursday.

"How can that be?" I cried.

McNally's shoulders seemed to sag. "Look, kid—I failed you. I didn't protect you from that Jordan twit. My boss is probably going to pull me off the job." He smiled, in a sad sort of way. "The weird thing is, I didn't want the job to begin with. I figured it was just sort of baby-sitting, you know. But I was getting to kind of like you." He sighed. "Maybe you'll be better off with someone else."

"But I don't want anyone else! You are my bodyguard. I want you to take care of me."

To tell you the truth—which I have been doing all along in these pages—I was surprised to hear myself say this. I did not realize how much I had come to depend on McNally until it looked as if I might lose him. Not in any specific way; I didn't look to him for answers, or information, or ideas. I just felt safer with him around. And not so lonely, somehow.

We rode to school in deep gloom.

When we entered the classroom, I was shocked to see that half the desks were empty. Even worse, most of the kids who *were* there wouldn't look at me.

Ms. Weintraub had the appearance of one who had not slept at all the night before.

I felt as if I had come from another planet or something.

Of course, I *had* come from another planet. But this was the first school where the kids had made me feel that way.

I didn't like it.

We started with reading group. I liked this part of class. I had picked up the basic ability to read this language from the training modules, but I had much to learn about the way people lived here, and stories are the best way to do that.

87

The kids who sat next to me in group looked very nervous. They edged away from me, as if I smelled bad.

I felt cold and small inside.

Halfway through the morning Ms. Weintraub gave us a short break. Kids got up and started to move around, getting drinks, talking to each other, things like that. At first no one came anywhere near me. Then the dark-haired boy that Jordan had called "Nerdbutt" the day before started in my direction.

Was he going to talk to me? I felt that was all I needed—just *one* person to come over and say I was all right.

Before he could reach my desk, someone knocked at the door.

"Come in," called Ms. Weintraub.

The door swung open. Mr. Grand entered, followed by four men in dark suits.

"We want to talk to Pleskit," said one of them.

McNally stood up. "You'll have to clear that with me, first."

"Got the clearance right here," said the guy, taking some papers out of his jacket pocket.

McNally went to look at the papers. "They're signed by Mikta-makta-mookta," he said, glancing at me.

"The secretary of the Fatherly One has power to grant such permission," I said, making the smell of reluctant acceptance.

Three kids pinched their noses.

McNally looked back at the men. "No offense, fellas, but I want to double-check this." He reached into his own pocket and pulled out a scanner. I recognized it as having come from the embassy. He ran it over the paper, which began to glow.

He sighed. "It's genuine. Better go with them, Pleskit."

"Will you come, too?"

"Of course!" said McNally.

"No," said the lead guy. "Just the boy."

McNally shook his head. "You take Pleskit, you get me, too. We come as a package."

"You're not authorized for this, McNally," growled the lead guy.

"I'm not authorized to let the boy out of my sight."

"You should have remembered that yesterday!"

McNally's eyes flashed. But he didn't respond to the insult. He just said, "Take Pleskit, take me. Don't want me, leave the kid here."

"This could cost you your job."

"I wouldn't be doing my job if I let him go without me."

"It's your head," said the guy, making a shrug.

McNally nodded to me, and I came to stand beside him.

Together, we followed the four men out of the room.

CHAPTER
15
[TIM]

Personal Needs Chamber

When Mrs. Vanderhof drove Linnsy and me to school on Thursday morning, things were even worse than they had been the first day. A huge crowd of people lined the street, almost all of them carrying anti-alien signs. I recognized several parents among the crowd—and even a handful of kids.

The protesters had put up a podium where Senator Hargis was making a raving, totally nasty speech. He was giving the crowd a good dose of Vitamin Hate, and they were eating it up.

Since it took even longer to get through the police barricade than it had the first day, we got to hear some of Hargis's pep rally of hate.

"These aliens are anti-American!" he was bellowing when we first pulled up. "Who do they think they are, coming here with their strange ideas, their interplanetary germs, their pulsating head knobs? We have to root them out, send them back to where they came from! They're a danger, a menace! They're monsters, I tell you. *Monsters!* Why, poor Jordan here was almost killed by one of them yesterday."

That was when I realized he had Jordan on the platform with him! He even asked the little creep to make a speech about what had happened to him.

"I was just talking to Pleskit," said Jordan, "trying to make friends, you know? Then all of a sudden that purple knob on the top of his head blasted out a ray of power and knocked me unconscious!"

"Just talking!" I muttered to Linnsy. "What a liar!"

"It was the most terrifying thing that ever happened to me," continued Jordan. He sounded like he was about to cry.

"He is a pretty good actor, though," said Linnsy.

"Yeah. If they give an Academy Award for best performance as a butthead, he'll be sure to win."

Then, to my astonishment, Jordan actually said something that made me happy.

"I won't be able to go back to school until that menace is gone," he whined, his voice quivering. "I won't feel safe in my own classroom!"

I haven't felt safe in my own classroom since you came here, Jordan, I thought. *Why should you be any different?*

"Let's have a big hand for this young hero!"

93

shouted Senator Hargis. "We owe him a vote of thanks for showing what a menace the aliens truly are!"

The audience burst into applause.

I groaned. "I think I'm going to throw up."

"Not in the car!" said Linnsy's mother.

I tried three times to talk to Pleskit that morning. The first two times I struck out because he got up to go to his Personal Needs Chamber.

McNally went with him both times. Suddenly I wondered if the bodyguard waited outside or actually went in with Pleskit. That would certainly mess up my plan—not that I had figured out how to get out of the classroom anyway.

The third time I was getting ready to try to talk to Pleskit, Mr. Grand showed up with a bunch of guys in black suits. When they took Pleskit out of the room, I almost screamed. It was like proof that there was no way I was ever going to get a chance to talk to him.

Then some worse thoughts occurred to me. What if things had gone so badly here they were planning to take him to some other school? Or, even worse, what if the aliens had just decided to leave the planet in disgust? Or—worst of all— what if our government had thrown them out?

I WAS A SIXTH GRADE ALIEN

I collapsed at my desk. In the distance Senator Hargis was still bellowing his message of fear.

As I sat there, wrapped in despair, someone slid a piece of paper under my arm.

Unfolding it, I tried not to let out a yelp of delight.

Linnsy had come through after all!

"Dear Ms. Weintraub," said the paper. "Please excuse Tim at 10:45 A.M., because I have to take him to the dentist."

It was signed, "Sincerely, Julie Tompkins."

The handwriting was clear and looked almost exactly like my mom's. That was because Linnsy and I had spent weeks trying to learn to sign her name a few years back, when we wanted to take out some video that the store wouldn't let us have without a permission slip. I was hopeless at it; my handwriting looks sort of like you rolled skinny worms in ink and let them thrash around on the page. But Linnsy had gotten really good at it.

I looked up at the clock. It was 10:40.

Time to get moving.

I had to interrupt a reading group to show the note to Ms. Weintraub, which is something she Does Not Like. She was also annoyed that I hadn't mentioned the dentist appointment earlier. But she was already used to the way I forget things, so she wasn't really suspicious.

I hurried out of the room, realized I had forgotten the key, and went back to my desk to get it.

Once I was back in the hall, I glanced both ways.

No one was coming. I hurried to Pleskit's Personal Needs Chamber and slipped the key into the lock—hoping they hadn't changed it when they redid the room.

Holding my breath, I turned it.

Bingo! The door opened, and I slipped inside.

I couldn't have gone to the bathroom in that place if I had had to pee so bad my hair was getting fertilized! I couldn't even figure out what most of the stuff was *for*—though I did like the black and pink wall that had water constantly running down its surface. In front of that was a strange device that looked like a metallic lizard; thick tubes that expanded into soft, blossom-like objects sprouted from its back. I had no idea what it was for, but I thought it was fascinating. On the other hand, the gurgling hole in the center of the floor kind of scared me.

Despite all my reading, despite how sure I had been that I could understand the aliens, this was the first time I understood how different they are from us.

I stationed myself against one of the dry walls and settled in to wait. Only I don't do so well at waiting, so my mind started to fuss about things. Like: *What if Pleskit isn't coming back?* Or *What if he does come back, but McNally comes in the room with him?* Would the bodyguard think I was a dangerous intruder? Would he *shoot* at me?

I wished I had worn my watch. I had planned to, only I hadn't been able to find it for the last week.

I started to wonder if the room was soundproof. What if hours had gone by, and everyone had left? What if I was alone in the school?

What happens in a place like this at night?

Maybe my mother was already in a state of major fuss, wondering what had happened to me.

Pretty soon I had myself in such a dither that when I heard the door open, it was all I could do to keep from screaming.

CHAPTER
16
[PLESKIT]

A Glimmer of Light

The men took me to an office near where Principal Grand works. We all sat at a long table, except for McNally, who stood a few feet behind me.

"So, Plastic, what do you call that thing on top of your head?" asked the man who seemed to be in charge of the group.

I decided to give him the full name. "It is called a sphen-<double knuckle pop>-gnut-[small, non-smelly fart]-ksher."

The man gave me a funny look. "How do you use it?"

"What is this all about?" asked McNally before I could answer.

"Shut up, McNally," said one of the other men. "We've got authorization to question the boy."

McNally made a kind of growling sound but didn't say anything else.

The man repeated his question. "How do you use it?"

"I do not know how to answer that. I do not think about using it, any more than I think about how I use my breathing sac, or my food-masher, or my *clinkus*. It just does its job."

"Well, what *is* its job?" asked the man.

"To gather energy and focus it for future use," I said. I did not add that it also records all I experience during a day so I can study what has happened, and learn from my mistakes.

"Can you shoot it at people?" asked another of the men.

"Shoot it?" I replied, puzzled by the question.

"Like a gun."

I actually laughed, which I probably should not have done. "The sphen-gnut-ksher emits energy to protect me if I am in danger. I cannot use it as an aggressive weapon. That would be silly."

"Yeah, Mortenson," said another of the men, smiling. "That would be silly."

"What's this all about, anyway?" asked McNally again.

"Shut up, McNally," said several of the men.

"Please do not talk to Mr. McNally that way," I said. "He is my friend, and that is disrespectful."

"Yeah," said McNally with a smile. "It's disrespectful."

The leader rolled his eyes, then asked me the next question. But he kept coming back to the *sphen-gnut-ksher*. As near as I could make out, what they really wanted to know was how dangerous it was, and whether there was some way they could make one for themselves.

It seemed like forever before one of them said, "I think that's about enough for now. Thanks for the information, Pleskit. You can return to your room now."

I was exhausted, and somewhat cranky. The whole episode had been so upsetting that I had to *finussher.*

"I need to stop at my Personal Needs Chamber," I told McNally as we were walking back to the classroom.

"I understand completely," he said. He sounded a little uncomfortable himself.

He took the key from his pocket and unlocked the door. Then he positioned himself next to it while I went into the chamber. As I went around the sight barrier, into the main space, I was astonished to find one of my classmates standing near the *whizzoria*.

"What are you doing here?" I asked angrily. My *sphen-gnut-ksher* was starting to sizzle.

"Don't zap me!" he cried, diving behind the *whizzoria*.

I sighed. "I am not going to zap you, Nerdbutt. I just want to be alone so I can *finussher!*"

He looked surprised, and a little sad. "Maybe the others are right after all," he said, half to himself.

"Right about what?"

"That you're a stuck-up snot."

"Why do you say that?" I cried.

"Why did you call me Nerdbutt?" he countered.

This confused me. "Isn't that your name?"

"Yeah, right," he said.

"So it *is* your name," I said, more confused than ever.

"Of course it's not my name! It's just something that Jordan likes to call me."

"Oh, Jordan," I said. "The nasty one."

"That's him," said the intruder. "Look, I just

101

wanted to talk to you for a minute. I've been trying to ever since you got here, but there's always someone around you, or you're getting pulled away to talk to someone, or you're coming in here. I was afraid you might leave for good before I even had a chance to say hello, and I've been waiting all my life to meet someone like you. I'll go away right now, if you want me to. I just had to tell you that not everyone is upset that you're here. I think it's the most exciting thing that ever happened, and I'd really, *really* like to be friends!"

Given what had happened to me so far, it was hard to be mad at someone who simply wanted to be friends—even if he had invaded my privacy.

"What is your real name?" I asked.

"Tim Tompkins," he said, putting out his hand.

My training modules had prepared me for this ritual. "I am Pleskit Meenom, childling of Meenom Ventrah, childling of Ventrah Komquist," I replied, leaving out the smells and body sounds I would have added for someone who had full use of his senses.

We grasped hands and shook.

"You know, you will probably get in trouble for coming in here," I said.

Tim made that up and down shoulder motion Earthlings call a shrug. "I'm used to getting in trouble. And this used to be my hangout, before they put in all the fancy plumbing. How do you use this stuff, anyway?"

"That is a very private question!"

Tim, whose face is usually pink, turned red.

"That's amazing!" I cried. "How did you do that?"

"Do what?"

"Turn red like that. What a good trick!"

"It's just a blush," said Tim, becoming even redder than he was already.

"Can you teach me to do it? It would probably make the Fatherly One fall over!"

"I don't think I can teach you," said Tim Tompkins. "It's just something you do when you're embarrassed."

"I did not mean to embarrass you," I said urgently.

"Don't worry about it. Happens all the time."

"But I thought it was a great crime to embarrass someone—almost as bad as not speaking the absolute truth."

Tim burst into laughter.

"What is so funny?" I asked.

"The idea that we always tell the absolute truth! People here lie all the time! What made you think we don't?"

I could not answer. I was seized by horror.

Finally I began to understand what had been happening to me.

CHAPTER
17
[TIM]

Buddies

Pleskit began to sway. A terrible odor came from the knob on top of his head.

"Are you all right?" I cried.

"How can I be all right? I have been betrayed!"

"What are you talking about?"

"My training modules did not tell me the truth!" A bitter new scent filled the air. "They were lying about the truth, Tim! That was why I said those terrible things my first day here—my training modules had taught me that Earthlings value the absolute truth above all else."

"Are you kidding? We *live* on little white lies."

Pleskit slid to the floor. Even though he was in a sitting position, he was so quiet that for a minute

I was afraid he had fainted, or had a heart attack, or something. I figured I was going to have to go for help. This idea was not all that appealing, since it would mean admitting I had been in Pleskit's bathroom instead of at the dentist's.

Just as I was heading for the door, he opened his eyes and took a deep breath. "Would you like to come home with me this afternoon?" he asked.

My first impulse was to scream, "ARE YOU KIDDING! I WOULD *LOVE* TO COME HOME WITH YOU! I'VE BEEN *DYING* TO SEE INSIDE WHERE YOU LIVE!!!!"

Fortunately, I managed not to do that. Fighting to keep my voice calm, I said, "Yeah, I'd like that. Thank you." But inside, I felt like I had fireworks going off in my brain.

It was one of the longer days of my life. After Pleskit went back to the classroom, I stayed in his Personal Needs Chamber for another hour and a half. After all, I was supposed to be at a dentist appointment. So I couldn't go back to the room right away. (It wasn't until later that I realized I could just have gone back and said the appointment had been canceled. I'm not real good at this sneaky stuff.)

Since I didn't have a watch, I had to wait for

Pleskit to come back and tell me when enough time had gone by.

I spent some time trying to figure out Pleskit's plumbing, of course. I couldn't make much sense of it, though. And when I tossed a wad of gum down that hole in the floor, it disappeared with a flash and a sizzle. So I decided not to try peeing down it, even though I really had to go.

To make things worse, I missed lunch. I was so hungry I felt like my belly button was kissing my backbone.

I decided to pretend I was a prisoner of a horrible intergalactic villain. Pressing myself against a wall, I imagined I was being held there by an unbreakable force field.

By the time Pleskit came in to tell me it was okay to go back to the classroom, I felt like both my head and my bladder were going to explode. (Even then I had to wait for him to go back to the room before I could come out, since we didn't want McNally to see the two of us leaving the Personal Needs Chamber together.)

All I could think about for the rest of the afternoon was going to Pleskit's place. I was so distracted I made three really stupid mistakes in math, which is normally one of my best subjects.

Also, I was pretty sure the clock had died altogether, since it took at least fourteen hours to go from 1:13 to 1:14.

I did get a note from Linnsy saying: "SO WHAT HAPPENED?!?!?!?!"

"Mission accomplished!" I wrote, and sent the note back.

She smiled and gave me the thumbs-up sign.

When the day finally ended, Pleskit motioned to me. I went to where he was standing. He introduced me to his bodyguard and said that I would be going home with them.

McNally nodded but didn't say anything.

Ms. Weintraub seemed pleased, and surprised, when we left the room together. Linnsy, however, looked jealous. I realized I was going to owe her one incredibly massive favor.

Pleskit's limousine was totally cool; the backseat alone was almost as big as my mother's whole car.

But the limo was nothing compared to the embassy. When we got there, a door opened in the ground, and we drove down a long ramp. Then we took this slick glass elevator up the "hook" (as Pleskit called the curving support piece) into the embassy itself.

"Shall we go to the kitchen for a snack?" asked Pleskit.

"Sounds great!" I said. "I'm starving!"

Immediately I wondered if I had just done something really stupid. What kind of "snack" had I let myself in for?

We went into the kitchen, and I screamed.

Man, I have *never* felt so stupid! I mean, I thought I was so cool about aliens and stuff, but when I finally met a truly weird one face to face, it just wigged me out for a minute.

"Are you all right?" asked Pleskit, looking very concerned. "Oh, good. You're doing that trick where you turn red! I hoped you would show that to Shhh-foop."

I figured out that by "Shhh-foop" he meant the creature who was sliding across the floor to greet me. She looked like a six-foot-tall bunch of spotted orange celery with an octopus growing out of its top. "Greetings, Mr. Timothy!" she sang in an amazingly beautiful voice. Then she extended a tentacle to me.

Cautiously, I reached out and took the tentacle. "Greetings," I replied, trying not to squeak.

She squeezed my hand, leaving only a trace of slime.

"I was just making some *finnikle-pokta*," she sang. (According to Pleskit, she always sings; it must be like living in an opera.) "Would you boys like some?"

"We sure would!" cried Pleskit eagerly.

"Uh . . . sure," I said, torn between hunger and terror.

"Cup of coffee, Mr. McNally?" sang Shhh-foop.

"How is it today?" asked McNally, sounding uncertain.

"New recipe," sang Shhh-foop. She slid across the floor and whacked a pair of tentacles against a smooth countertop. Up popped a steaming pot of coffee. She poured a cup and brought it to McNally, who looked at it nervously.

Pleskit and I sat down at the table. I yelped again when the chair started shifting under my butt.

Pleskit smiled. "Do not be alarmed. It is simply adjusting to make you more comfortable."

He was right. In about thirty seconds it was the most comfortable chair I had ever sat in.

Just then a door slid open and someone else came into the room. He was green, a little over four feet tall, and probably almost that big across the center. He had on a skin-tight red suit with a broad yellow strip around the center. It made him look like a beach ball with arms and legs.

"Greetings, Barvgis!" said Pleskit. "Come meet Tim Tompkins from my class in school."

As Barvgis came closer I could see that his skin was covered with slime. I tried to stay cool about it, but it wasn't easy. My mother used to call her old boss a slimeball, but that was just because of the way he acted. This guy really *was* a slimeball!

It turned out that he was also nice and friendly. He wanted to practice telling me Earth jokes—which he then asked me to explain to him.

While we were talking, Shhh-foop slid over to the table carrying a tray in her tentacles. It was made of blue metal and had a rim that looked almost like a fence. Piled on top of the tray were the *finnikle-pokta*. (That's what you call a bunch of them; just one is a *fin-pok*.) About the size of walnuts, they looked like a cross between a honeycomb and a sponge. They came in several bright colors. And they all had stuff oozing out of the holes.

"Yum!" cried Pleskit, grabbing one and popping it into his mouth. "I love these things!"

War had broken out in my stomach. Part of it was crying "FEED ME! I AM STARVING!" An-

other part was screaming "DON'T YOU DARE TRY SENDING ONE OF THOSE THINGS DOWN HERE!"

One *fin-pok* squeaked and rolled across the plate.

"Hurry," said Pleskit. "They're best when they're fresh."

It wasn't hunger that got me to eat one. It was the fact that I would have had to consider myself a failure and a fraud if, after all this time of wanting to meet aliens, I had been afraid to try the first piece of food they offered me.

So I reached out and took one.

Trying to describe it would be like trying to describe a totally new color, a color that wasn't like any other color you had ever seen. I simply don't have the right words. Let's just say that the *fin-pok* seemed to find parts of my tongue I hadn't even known existed. Some of them were happy to be found, some were not.

I ate six *finnikle-pokta* in all—two red, two green, two purple. Each had its own specific taste.

"Good, huh?" said Pleskit, wiping juice from his chin.

"Fascinating," I replied, with absolute honesty.

On the other side of the room I noticed

McNally pouring his coffee into something I figured must be a sink.

Shhh-foop saw him, too. "Alas, alas," she sang in a voice so sad it almost made me cry. "Once again Shhh-foop has failed to properly honor the bean of caffeine."

"Don't worry, Shhh-foop," said McNally. "You'll get it right one of these days. I'm going to my room, guys. See you later."

I started to ask Pleskit why his bodyguard could leave him. Then I realized that—of course—McNally wouldn't need to be on duty *in* their home. The embassy probably had better security systems than Fort Knox.

After our snack Pleskit wanted to introduce me to his dad, or The Fatherly One, as he called him.

We took the elevator to the next level of the embassy.

"First we have to get past his secretary," said Pleskit as we went through an oval door. The room we entered, blue and shaped like an egg, had a round desk mounted about halfway up the wall. Sitting behind the desk was an alien who made me think of an overgrown hamster. She was wearing a tight red outfit and stuffing something into her cheek as we came in.

"Greetings, Mikta-makta-mookta," said Pleskit. "This is my friend, Tim."

"Greetings, Tim," said Mikta-makta-mookta pleasantly. "I am very pleased to meet you."

"Is the Fatherly One available?" asked Pleskit.

"Alas, no. He has agreed to have a televised debate with the despicable Senator Hargis tonight. He is hoping to undo some of the damage that you—"

She stopped, as if she had said something she shouldn't. I glanced at Pleskit. He looked terrible.

"He is hoping to smooth things over with the people of Earth," said Mikta-makta-mookta.

"I will wait and speak to him later," said Pleskit.

I followed him out of the room.

"We must talk to *someone* about the training modules," he said. "Perhaps we should visit the Grandfatherly One."

"You brought your grandfather along?" I asked in surprise.

"Well, not the total Grandfatherly One. He died before I was born. But we've still got his brain. Let's go hear what it has to say."

CHAPTER
18
[PLESKIT]

The Grandfatherly One's Brain

Tim looked horrified and his voice sounded unusually squawky as he cried, "You kept your grandfather's brain after he died?"

Before I could answer, he closed his eyes. I could smell just the tiniest hint of embarrassment—the first time I realized that Earthlings have any ability to communicate by smell. When he opened his eyes again, I could tell he was trying to be calm. "That's very interesting," he said. "It is not a custom that we follow."

"Perhaps you do not have the right technology," I said.

"I'm sure we don't," replied Tim.

"Well, come along. I will introduce you to the Venerated One. You'll be his first Earthling!"

We keep the brain of the Grandfatherly One in a small room located between the living area and the business area. The room is quiet and peaceful. ("Boring," is how the Grandfatherly One describes it.)

Tim kept looking around as I led him to that room, going "Wow!" and "Cool!" as we passed different areas. But when we got to the room of the Grandfatherly One, my new friend just stood and stared for a while. Finally he said, *"That's your grandfather?"*

The brain of the Grandfatherly One resides in a clear vat. The vat is filled with an electrolyte solution that keeps him comfortable. Mounted on the sides of the vat are a pair of speakers that allow him to express his thoughts.

"I am what's *left* of Pleskit's Grandfatherly One," he said. "Should have let go of this life long ago, but Meenom asked me to stay around to advise him. As his Fatherly One, I felt I had to. Not that he ever actually asks for my advice."

"You speak English?" asked Tim in astonishment.

"I don't speak at all, when you come right

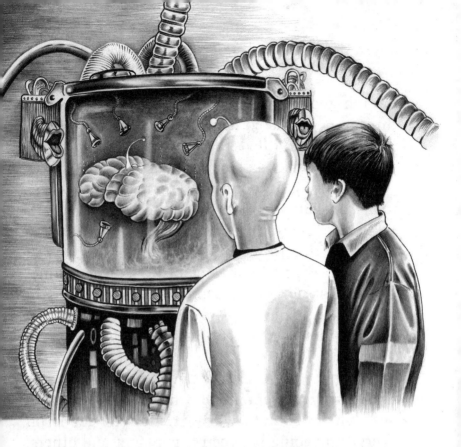

down to it. Just send my thoughts to the little boxes on the side of this body substitute, and they do the speaking. When we decided to settle here, Meenom had the computer processor changed so I could express myself in English—as if I ever had the chance or the need! So, what brings you here, anyway, Pleskit? And who's your friend?"

"This is Tim Tompkins, O Venerated One. He is in my class at school. He gave me some information today that helped me understand why things have gone so badly for me so far."

Quickly we filled the Venerated One in on what had happened since my arrival.

"Something is definitely *skigpoo* in *Gulzee-mia*," he said when we were finished.

"But I still don't understand *why* someone would do this to me," I said.

"Don't whine!" he snapped. "Never whine. Think instead. The reasons are obvious if you follow the money."

"The money?" asked Tim, sounding puzzled. "What money?"

"Meenom is here on a trade mission. He gets only a tiny percentage of whatever trade develops, but as Founding Trader, he will get it on *everything* going between this planet and others. If Earth turns out to be a good trade center, his profits could be stupendous. Unless . . ."

"Unless *what?*" I cried.

"Unless he is removed from the mission—in which case whoever develops the trade instead will receive that money."

"But we don't know if we're going to be able to find anything tradeworthy," I said.

"Think!" repeated the Grandfatherly One. "Just because you don't know something, doesn't mean someone else doesn't. Anyone who did would have a powerful motive for sabotaging the mission of your Fatherly One. The more valuable the item, the more powerful the motive."

"I don't get it," said Tim. "How would anyone else know something like that?"

The Grandfatherly One snorted, a sound he likes to make no matter what language his container is programmed for. "Just because this planet is restricted doesn't mean other members of the federation haven't been down here poking around. Let's assume that's the case and someone wants to ruin the mission. So they think, 'All right, what's the best way to get at Meenom?' And the answer is, through his soft spot—which is you, Pleskit. Certainly you have a record for causing problems, especially after Geembol Seven."

Tim glanced at me. I wanted to tell the Grandfatherly One to drop it, but feared that if I did he wouldn't tell me the other things I wanted to know. So I interrupted with a question.

"What should we *do?*"

"I think you boys need to do some investigating."

"Can't you just tell the Fatherly One what is going on?"

"I would if I could get his attention! I can't believe I came all this way to be ignored! I should have died and gotten it over with when I had the chance. Send him to me if you can find him. Send him right now, if you can."

"Alas, he is not here. He's going to be on television tonight with Senator Hargis, to debate the mission."

"Uh-oh," said the Grandfatherly One. "I hope he's not walking into a trap."

"Do you think he's in danger?" I cried.

"Not physical danger. But I wonder if his enemies have set this up with the intent of humiliating him."

"What can we do?" asked Tim.

"I already told you—start doing some investigating. After all, if the training modules *were* sabotaged, odds are good that it was an inside job."

"You mean someone within the embassy is trying to get me?"

"I'm just saying it's a possibility. Now look, if you two *do* go snooping around, for Gimblat's sake, be careful. Whoever is doing this is playing for big stakes."

"Thank you for your wisdom, O Venerated One," I said, bending my *sphen-gnut-ksher* toward his tank in a gesture of respect.

"Yeah, yeah, yeah. Now go on, will you? I need to take a nap. Space and stars, but I wish I had never agreed to postponing the final Death Trip. I get so tired these days. Probably because I can't exercise."

"It was a pleasure to meet you, sir," said Tim.

"Yeah, yeah, yeah. You seem like a nice kid. Don't let Pleskit get you into too much trouble."

CHAPTER
19
[TIM]

The Traitor

After we left Pleskit's grandfather, I said, "Okay, let's think about this. Who are the main suspects?"

"You and I," said Pleskit promptly.

"Huh?"

"You and I are the ones who suspect someone tampered with the modules."

This was going to be more difficult than I thought. "I mean, who are the people we have to be suspicious of? Everyone who works here, I suppose. How big is the embassy staff?"

"Just three. I already introduced you to them."

I looked at Pleskit in astonishment. "You only have three people to run this entire building?"

Pleskit looked as astonished as I felt. "Well, that's not counting McNally. Why would we need more?"

"So who does the cleaning, and stuff like that?"

Pleskit laughed. "The building cleans itself! It can cook, too, for that matter. We only brought Shhh-foop because the Fatherly One will need a real cook when he starts to host official dinners."

"How come the place is so big?" I asked, still confused. "You could have *twenty* people living here and they wouldn't bump into each other."

"The staff will expand if the mission is successful," said Pleskit. He paused, then added, "I think the building can expand, too, if we need it to."

"It must be fun to be an alien," I said, feeling jealous.

"Actually, so far, it has mostly meant being lonely," Pleskit replied, somewhat bitterly.

"Gee, thanks a lot."

"Do not be offended!" said Pleskit quickly. "I am speaking of what is past. The training modules did not warn me that your people are so sensitive."

"Well, speaking of those training modules, we have to figure out who was monkeying with

125

yours. Now if Barvgis, Shhh-foop, and Mikta-makta-mookta are our suspects, the next question is, who has a motive?"

"According to the Fatherly One, money is a motive for everyone," said Pleskit.

"Well, that doesn't do much to narrow things down. Hmmm. Do any of them particularly dislike your, uh, Fatherly One?"

"Not that I can think of. He is gruff, but fair."

I sighed. "Okay, scratch off motive. Let's move on to opportunity."

Pleskit looked at me strangely. "How do you know so much about this, Tim? Are you planning a life of crime?"

I almost got offended again, until I reminded myself that one reason I was interested in aliens was that they would be so different from us. Since we would be as different from them as they are from us, I shouldn't expect Pleskit to understand me automatically.

"I don't *ever* plan to commit a crime. I just read a lot of Hardy Boys books."

"Books about healthy boys talk about crime?"

I sighed. "The Hardy Boys are a team. Brothers. They *solve* crimes."

"Ahhh," said Pleskit. The purple knob on his head sent out an odor that made me think of clear stream water. At least, it did at first. Suddenly the smell turned rank and sour, like rotten cabbage mixed with chemical waste.

"Whooie, Pleskit!" I yelped, grabbing my nose to pinch it shut. "What does *that* mean?"

His face looked grim. "I have just realized at whom the fateful finger of suspicion should be pointing."

"Who?"

"Barvgis!"

"That slimy round guy? Why him?"

"Because he handles all official documents and materials. Therefore, he would have had the best chance to interfere with my training modules."

"But he was so nice," I said, not wanting to believe it.

"The Fatherly One taught me long ago that sometimes nice people are truly nice, and sometimes they are the ones who are most *skeezpul.*"

"What's *skeezpul?*"

Pleskit looked embarrassed. "Sorry. I did not mean to say that."

"But what does it mean?"

"I cannot tell you."

"Why? Is it like some top secret thing?"

"No."

"Well, then what is it?"

"A word so bad that it cannot be translated into your language."

"Cool!" I said. "What does it mean?"

Pleskit looked at me strangely. "I just told you, it cannot be translated."

"Oh. Yeah. Well, skip that. What are we going to do about Barvgis?"

"Let us enter his room to seek incriminating data."

"Won't he fry our butts if he catches us?"

Pleskit shuddered. "Why would he cook our hind ends? He is not an eater of intelligent beings."

"It's just an expression. I was saying that I'm afraid we could get in a lot of trouble."

"I already *am* in a lot of trouble."

Well, that was true. But *I* wasn't, at least, not yet. The thing was, if I was going to be Pleskit's buddy, I couldn't back out when he needed my help just because I was a little afraid. Besides, if Barvgis really had sabotaged Pleskit's training modules, he had done a truly horrible thing.

"Okay," I said. "Let's go."

Pleskit smiled at me. "Thanks, pal."

The staff living quarters were located in a long, smooth-sided hallway. I didn't realize the walls were smooth at first, because they looked like a living jungle—a *purple* living jungle. The effect was so real that when I first saw it, I reached out to touch one of the leaves; I was astonished when my hand hit a solid wall.

"Nice, isn't it," said Pleskit. "We change it every few days. This is a scene from a planet named . . ." He paused, then made a series of knuckle cracks, burped twice, and sent me a smell like overripe cherries. "Sorry," he said. "It's another one of those words that doesn't translate."

"It's awesome," I said as I watched an utterly strange creature swing through the trees in the distance.

"The room of Barvgis is here," said Pleskit, leading me down the hall. Suddenly he stopped. His eyes went wide. The knob on his head made a smell that even I could tell meant raw terror.

CHAPTER
20
[PLESKIT]

Snooping

"He's coming!" I whispered to Tim.

"Who?"

"*Barvgis!*"

Tim did that trick of changing color again, only this time he turned almost pure white. "How do you know?" he hissed.

"Can't you smell him?"

"Of course not!"

This was no time to discuss the inadequacies of an Earthling's nasal equipment. "Come on," I said. "We've got to get out of here." I pulled him toward a door on the other side of the hall.

"It's locked!" said Tim. His voice was low, desperate.

I cracked my knuckles at the door, then pushed it open.

"How did you do that?"

"It's a combination lock. Come on. And be quiet!"

We slipped inside and closed the door carefully behind us. Once we were inside, I felt better. "That was a close one," I said, leaning against the door.

The room was dark, almost cavelike. A warm, woody smell filled the air. The far wall, about ten feet away from us, had three doors.

"Where . . . where are we?" asked Tim.

"These are the rooms of Mikta-makta-mookta. We should be safe here—unless she comes in, of course. Her people are quite ferocious about their privacy."

Tim groaned. "How will we know when Barvgis is gone?"

"We'll just give him time to get into his room. We'll have to come back later, but—"

I stopped speaking.

"What?" said Tim. "What is it?"

"That should not be here!"

"What? What shouldn't be here?"

"That," I said, moving toward one of the three doors. On the far side of it was a glassy tube, capped with green metal beautifully shaped into the form of a kibooble vine. The tube was about three feet wide and stood nearly as tall as the ceiling.

"What is it?" asked Tim, following closely at my heels.

"A transporter."

"You mean like 'Beam me up, Scottie'? You guys really have those things?"

I turned toward him. "Sometimes I feel as if we are not speaking the same language. Aren't Scotties something you use to wipe your nose?"

Tim shook his head. "Never mind that. Can this take a person from one place to another?"

"Precisely!" I said, pleased that he had figured it out so quickly. "It's an elevator, and it transports people."

"An *elevator?*" He sounded disappointed.

"Yes. You know, for going up and down in. Only there should not be a private one in this room. It is against—"

I stopped, struck silent by terror, as a light began to glow on the top of the tube.

"What's the matter?" asked Tim.

"Someone is coming! Hide. *Hide!*"

"Where?" squeaked Tim.

I spun around, looking for somewhere, any-

where, that we could get out of sight. In the far corner I saw a large brown sphere with a small opening in the front. "In there!" I hissed, grabbing Tim's arm and pulling him toward it.

He followed me through the opening. It was dark and cozy inside.

"What is this place?" he whispered.

"Mikta-makta-mookta's bed. Now be quiet!"

Cautiously I moved my head so that one eye could just barely see out of the bed's entrance hole. Tim positioned himself at the other side of the hole.

So we both saw the figure that arrived in the elevator.

It was Senator Hargis.

"Holy Moses!" whispered Tim. "What's *he* doing here?"

"I do not have the slightest idea." I was trying to decide whether we should step out and challenge him. But in that same instant I heard the outer door slide open.

I expected Senator Hargis to look frightened, maybe even try to hide. I half expected him to dive into the bed where Tim and I were!

But he just stood there, smiling.

I considered jumping out to warn Mikta-makta-mookta, even though doing so would reveal our hiding place. Tim must have sensed that, because he grabbed my arm and shook his head. I realized he was right. That private elevator wasn't supposed to be here to begin with. So the odds were good that anyone who came up in it had been invited by Mikta-makta-mookta herself.

"Harr-giss!" she cried. "What are you doing here?"

Before he could answer, she ran to him and threw her arms around him. They began to kiss, which surprised me so much that I let out a gasp.

"What was that?" cried Mikta-makta-mookta.

Senator Hargis started to sniff. He turned his head from side to side, very slowly. When he stopped, he was staring at the bed in which Tim and I were hiding.

"Whatever it was came from in there!" he said.

He began walking toward us.

CHAPTER
21
[TIM]

Evil Plan

Icy terror gripped my heart. Pleskit and I slid away from the opening of the bed, trying not to make a sound. But the wood shavings Mikta-makta-mookta used as her mattress rustled slightly as we moved through them.

A moment later Senator Hargis thrust his head through the opening of the bed. His eyes were hard, his voice cold as he asked, "What are you little *gnerfs* doing here?"

That was when the truth about Senator Hargis really sank in on me. *He was another alien!* I wondered if he had replaced the real Senator Hargis, or if had he been here in disguise for many years.

136

"Climb out of there, Pleskit," said the senator. "Let's see who you've got with you."

For a minute I hoped Pleskit might zap Hargis, the way he had Jordan. When he didn't, I wondered if it was because he was afraid, or because he knew that Hargis would be shielded against it.

"Sorry, Tim," whispered Pleskit as we met at the opening. "I did not mean to get you into so much trouble!"

I wanted to say something cool and slick, to show I wasn't worried. Too terrified to think of anything like that, I just nodded.

As I climbed out of the bed, Senator Hargis slapped something cold against the back of my neck. It stung. I tried to reach back to touch it, to pull it off. To my horror, I found that my arms would not obey my command.

Hargis laughed. I saw that he had a small black box in his hand, something that looked like a control panel.

"Just what are you two doing in my private quarters?" demanded Mikta-makta-mookta. She sounded as furious as I was frightened.

"It was an accident!" I said. "We were just trying to get away from Barvgis."

She wiggled her nose. "What does Barvgis have to do with this?"

"We thought he was the one who tampered with my training modules," Pleskit told her. "We wanted to check his room for evidence, but when we were at his door I smelled him coming. We ducked into your room to hide."

Mikta-makta-mookta made a sour chuckling sound. "So you stumbled onto the truth by accident."

"An unfortunate accident for them," said Harr-giss. "We cannot afford to let them live with this information."

I moved to a point beyond terror. "Nooooo!" I screamed. I tried to fling myself to the floor, and found that I couldn't—which only made me all the more frightened. "No No No NO NO! You can't kill us!"

"Oh, shut up, you little nitwit," said Mikta-makta-mookta, sounding weary. "We're not going to kill you. What kind of savages do you think we are? Great Mook, Harr-giss, do you think it's worth what we'll have to put up with to exploit this planet even if we do wrest it from Meenom's control?"

I stood still (I seemed to have no choice) feeling astonished, relieved, and slightly offended. "If you're not going to kill us, what *are* you going to do?" I asked.

Harr-giss gave me a nasty smile. "We're going to wipe your brains, you silly little Earthling."

I clutched my head in terror. "You're going to make me stupid?"

"Someone already beat us to it," said Mikta-makta-mookta. "What we're going to do now is give you a clean slate. You won't remember a thing when we're done, not even your name. You'll be able to start over again. Don't think of it as losing your mind, think of it as being given a second chance at childhood. Maybe you can do a better job of it the second time around. Of course, since we're only resetting your mind, in about ten years you'll have the brain of a child in the body of a man. However that seems to be a very common condition on this planet, so you should fit right in."

I started to tremble. I actually like being a kid. But the idea of starting again from scratch at the age of eleven was pretty terrifying. My mother would take care of me, of course. But the idea that I would not recognize her the next time I saw her, that I would never have a real memory of my father, gripped my throat.

"This is a vile crime you are contemplating," said Pleskit.

"Yes, it is," said Harr-giss. "But don't worry.

139

You won't remember a thing about it. So you'll have no idea why your Fatherly One holds such a bitter grudge against you when he is raising you for a second time."

"Why will he hold a grudge against *me?*" asked Pleskit.

"Oh, you silly boy," said Mikta-makta-mookta. "The whole point of this is to destroy his mission. We're not going to simply erase your and Tim's memories. We're going to make it look as if the entire horrible accident was *your* fault!"

"It's not hard to imagine the scenario," said Harr-giss. "When they find the two of you lying dazed and senseless, attached to a piece of technology you should never have touched, everyone will assume that you lured this pathetic Earthling into some mind experiment and accidentally wiped clean both his brain and yours. We'll work out the details later. Mikta can leak them to the press. They'll eat it up."

I groaned at the thought of eating anything. Between the fear and the *finnikle-pokta,* my stomach was in an uproar.

Harr-giss chuckled, perhaps the scariest sound I had ever heard. "Of course, with luck, I'll have already put an end to the mission myself by the time I'm done debating Meenom tonight. Everyone who thought 'Senator Hargis' was such a yokel alarmist will have to think again when I show them the footage I have from Geembol Seven."

"You wouldn't!" cried Pleskit, sounding horrified.

"Are you kidding?" replied Harr-giss. "I can't wait!"

"How are you going to explain having it?" asked Pleskit.

Harr-giss shrugged. "I'll say it was smuggled out to me by a source at the White House, someone concerned because the public wasn't getting the whole truth. The president will protest, of course—as well he might, since it will be a total lie. But no one will believe him. Since your news media have destroyed the credibility of everyone in power, my lies will be at least as believable as their truth."

He turned to Mikta-makta-mookta and handed her the control device. "I must leave for my debate with Meenom. I really just stopped by to get a kiss for luck. But this little visit turned out to be even luckier than I thought. I had figured that even after tonight it would take a while to end the mission. But this will give us a perfect one-two punch. First I reveal what happened on Geembol Seven. Then you 'discover' poor Pleskit and Tim with their brains wiped clean."

"It's too bad we have to do a mind wipe on Pleskit, too," said Mikta-makta-mookta.

I wondered if she was being sympathetic, or maybe just anti-Earthling, until Harr-giss said, "You're right; it would create even more of a backlash if it was only the Earth boy who got it. Well, we can't have everything—and we certainly can't have Pleskit remembering any of this. But here's an idea. When you 'discover' them, call for help from that bodyguard McNally. That way you'll have an Earthling witness. It'll play better on the news."

He turned back to Pleskit and me. "This really is quite delicious, boys. Though you would never know it from the pathetic way they refuse to spend reasonable money on medicine and educa-tion, Earthlings have a sentimental attachment to children. This incident will have billions of people demanding that Meenom be sent packing. As 'Senator Hargis,' I plan to play their fear like a Pesgallian concert master. We may actually get worldwide riots out of this!"

He gave Mikta-makta-mookta another kiss.

"Farewell, my little cheeble-cheeks," he said. Then he stepped into the elevator and disappeared.

Mikta-makta-mookta turned to us. Her beady eyes glittering, she said, "Okay, boys—time to kiss your brains good-bye."

CHAPTER
22
[P L E S K I T]

The Tech Room

When Mikta-makta-mookta turned her attention back to us, I could not help but emit the smell of bitterness. "You were the one who messed with my training modules, weren't you?"

"Of course," she said with a smile. She cracked a mook pod and stuffed the meat into her cheek. "You're so idealistic, Pleskit. I knew you would fall for that nonsense about Earthlings putting a high value on absolute truth." She chuckled. "Actually, it's the best way in the world to offend the silly creatures."

"I thought we were friends!" I cried.

"Oh, don't be silly. I was just using you. You already have a flair for getting into trouble. I knew it wouldn't take much help from me for you to mess up this mission so badly that your father would be recalled—though I must say this latest twist is beyond my fondest hopes. It will take a year or so for things to calm down enough for us to reestablish contact with Earth, of course. But Harr-giss is next in line with a claim, so all we have to do is wait. Then the rules of trade will leave the planet in our control. There won't be any of that benevolent partnership nonsense your goody-goody father is so fond of. We plan to really squeeze the place."

"You can't do that!" cried Tim.

"Of course we can," said Mikta-makta-mookta. "As Pleskit could have told you if he had wanted to, this planet is classified as 'Borderline Savage.' How it is managed is completely up to the trader who holds the primary claim. Meenom Ventrah had his style. Harr-giss and I have ours."

Tim moaned. Though I could not turn toward him because of the control disk on my neck, I could see him from the corner of my eye. He had already demonstrated that he could turn red and turn white. Now, to my astonishment, he looked slightly green.

I wondered just how many colors he was capable of.

"The question now," said Mikta-makta-mookta, "is how to get you to the Tech Room. It would be easiest just to make you walk there. But there's always the danger of running into some-one along the way." She looked around the room for a minute, her nose twitching. Then her beady eyes brightened. "Ah, *that's* it!"

She made an adjustment to the control box. I felt my throat tighten, and I could tell that I had lost the ability to speak. Another adjustment and I crumpled to the floor.

Tim landed with a thump beside me.

From where we lay I could see Mikta-makta-mookta walk to the other side of the room. She pulled a couple of large purple bags from a hole in the wall. I recognized them at once: laundry bags.

She stuffed Tim in one bag, me in the other. Chittering contentedly to herself, she tied the bags at the top.

I longed to lash out at her, to strike her with my fists, to shrivel her with words of scorn. Alas, my tongue was tied, as were my hands, by the control disk on the back of my neck.

Once she had us in the bags, Mikta-makta-mookta left the room. I desperately wanted to talk to Tim. I couldn't, of course, because of the control disk.

My questions about what Mikta-makta-mookta was doing were answered when I heard the door open once more. This was followed by the slight swish of a floating cart as it entered the room. Mikta-makta-mookta hoisted the bag I was in onto the top shelf of the cart—no problem for her, because she was very strong. I assume she put Tim on the bottom shelf.

When Mikta-makta-mookta untied the bag and pulled me out, we were in the Tech Room. I had not brought Tim here before, because it is off limits for Earthlings. The shelves and storage bins are filled with all the devices we anticipated needing in our first few years on the planet— everything from flying packs to tentacle straighteners.

"No one will have any trouble believing the Earth boy wanted to see this place," said Mikta-makta-mookta, glancing around. "Or that you were able to lure him here. We'll have to work on your motive, of course, though youthful stupidity will probably suffice. The more imaginative newspapers will probably label you 'The Death-wish Alien' or something. Ah, here they are!"

Though I could not see them from where I was lying, I knew what she was referring to: a pair of helmets, bright red and covered with many spiky little towers. They were extremely powerful, and extraordinarily dangerous. Used properly, they could transfer information from one brain to another, or temporarily enhance the power of someone's brain.

Used improperly, they could erase the contents of a brain the way you humans erase a computer disk.

"All right," she said cheerfully, "let's see what the best way to arrange this is. Pleskit, stand up." As she said this she made an adjustment to the control panel, freeing my body enough so that I could do as she commanded.

"Now you, Tim Tompkins," she said.

A moment later Tim was facing me.

He did not look well. His face was still another color, a kind of ashy gray this time.

Mikta-makta-mookta turned us so that we were standing side by side. Then she placed one of the helmets on my head, the other on Tim's. Though I could not move my muscles, I could still feel my body. A deep and sinking fear was moving in my guts, terror for myself, for the Fatherly One, and for the planet we had hoped to do so much to help.

Mikta-makta-mookta picked up the controls

for the helmets, which were connected by coiling wires.

If only I could lunge forward, strike the control panel from her hand. But though Mikta-makta-mookta was no more than two steps away, she might as well have been on another planet. I thought I would explode from the effort of trying to move.

Her beady eyes glittered at me. "I never did like you, Pleskit," she said as she put her hand on the dial.

Sick with fear, I prepared to have my memory erased.

Then Tim did something astonishing.

CHAPTER
23
[TIM]

Eruption

All right, I admit it. I saved the world by projectile vomiting.

Shhh-foop's *finnikle-pokta* had been rumbling around in my stomach ever since I ate them. I might have been able to keep them down, if we hadn't gotten in such terrible trouble. But from the time we slipped into Mikta-makta-mookta's room, I had been getting more and more tense.

By the time Harr-giss started talking about wiping out our memories, I had a small war going on down there. And while the disk he had slapped on the back of my neck controlled my voluntary movements, I guess it didn't have any effect on my body's *in*voluntary functions. My heart kept beating. My lungs kept breathing. And my stomach kept *trying* to digest. But finally it gave up the battle.

Since Mikta-makta-mookta was standing right in front of me when my insides erupted, I spewed a stream of red, green, and purple puke directly into her face.

It may not have been classy, but it was effective. She squealed in disgust and dropped the control pad as she tried to wipe her eyes. The pad bounced on the floor. That must have shifted its settings, because I could feel my muscles loosen the instant it landed. Unfortunately, I was too sick to do anything other than drop to my knees and puke again. Pleskit, on the other hand, dived for the control pad. I was still retching, and Mikta-makta-mookta was still wiping barf out of her eyes, when he pulled the control disk off my neck and slapped it onto the back of hers.

"Stand up!" he ordered in a furious voice.

And she stood.

I heaved—a sigh of relief this time. Then I staggered to my feet myself.

"That was an astonishing trick," said Pleskit as he pulled the control disk from the back of his own neck. "I did not know you could do anything like that. But stars above, what an odor!

It's like trying to smell a dictionary all at once. I can hardly think!"

"Well, I can. And what I think is, we've got to get to the studio before Harr-giss shows that video he's going to surprise your father with. If he convinces the world you guys should be thrown off the planet, it won't make any difference to anyone except us that we stopped Mikta-makta-mookta. Harr-giss and his gang will still end up running the world."

"You're right!" cried Pleskit. He looked down at the control pad. "I am not an expert on using this thing. Let's just tie her up for now. We'll come back and get her later."

"Good idea."

Mikta-makta-mookta blistered our ears with some amazing curses until Pleskit figured out how to set the No Talking command.

We found some stretchy cord, some super-strong tape, and some wire. We used them all. For good measure, Pleskit set the control pad on Zero Movement—and then took it with him when we left the room.

"What do we do now?" I asked as we left the Tech Room.

"Stay here for a moment," said Pleskit. "I want

to get something. Then we'll look for my body-guard. He should be able to get us to the studio."

Pleskit returned a few minutes later with a small black box. "Come on," he said. "Let's get McNally."

This turned out to be tougher than I expected. Though McNally was living at the embassy, Pleskit had never actually been to his room. We must have checked twenty empty rooms before we found him. When we finally did locate his room, he was taking a nap and we had to pound on his door to wake him.

I have to say he woke up a lot faster than I do. Must have something to do with being a body-guard. Anyway, once we explained the situation to him, he grabbed his coat and his gun and hustled us down to the limousine.

When we got to the parking area, it turned out that Ralph the Driver was not around.

"Have to do it myself," said McNally, not sounding all that happy.

"Can't you drive?" asked Pleskit.

"Sure I can drive. I just never drove a car this big. Well, climb in, guys. We're off to the studio."

He hit a button. The door to the tunnel swung open. We raced up the ramp, tires screeching as we turned the corner.

Pleskit switched on the backseat television. It took only a moment to find a station broadcasting the debate. It was just starting.

"Hurry!" cried Pleskit urgently. "Hurry!"

McNally hit the gas and the limousine surged forward.

It was only a few miles to the temporary studio, so we got there really fast. Even so, every second was agony as we kept expecting Harr-giss to pull out the Geembol Seven cassette.

"What's on this videotape anyway?" I asked Pleskit.

He shook his head. "An unfortunate experience that—like the episode with Jordan—looks much worse than it really was. I do not wish to speak about it."

I bit back a nasty comment. Instead, I suggested a plan for what we should do when we got to the studio.

We both agreed it was a good idea. There was only one problem. After we came screeching into the studio parking lot and hurried over to the door, we found that it was locked.

We pounded on it.

No one answered.

Finally McNally found a buzzer and pressed it.

"Password?" asked a mechanical sounding voice.

"We don't have a password!" roared McNally. "We have an emergency!"

"That is not correct," said the voice. "Admission denied."

McNally said some very bad words.

Then he kicked the door.

"Leave the premises, or authorities will be summoned," said the voice.

"I *am* an authority!" screamed McNally.

Pleskit was starting to tremble. He looked truly terrified.

And then I saw the answer to our problem—or at least a potential answer. All we had to do was hope that guilt would work in our favor.

C h a p t e r
24
[P L E S K I T]

Face to Face

"Look!" cried Tim. "It's Kitty James!"

I was so distressed about being locked out of the studio that at first I did not know what he was talking about. Then I remembered who Kitty James was—that terrible woman who had interviewed me in such a friendly way, then betrayed me by broadcasting the scene of me laughing when McNally asked if Jordan was dead.

"I do not want to see her!"

"But she works here!" cried Tim. "She can get us in."

"Why would she do that?" I asked.

"Because it's a story. Besides, she owes you a favor."

Before I could say anything, he rushed over to Kitty James and started talking to her.

"Sure, I can get you in," she said when she came over to the door. "Trade. I get you in, you grant me another exclusive interview."

"After what you did to me last time?" I cried.

She looked at me for a moment, then sighed. "Oh, all right. I guess I owe you one. I'll get you in. You can decide on your own if you want to do the interview or not."

Leaning close to the door, she said, "Kitty James. 8641. Baconbreath." It clicked, and she pushed on it. The door opened into a small room with two stairways and three doors leading out of it.

I groaned. "Which way now?"

McNally grabbed Kitty James by the arm. "Get us to the room where Meenom and Hargis are debating, and I guarantee you'll be on the scene for the biggest story of the year."

"It's a deal!" she said. She started down the center hall.

"Faster!" cried McNally.

Kitty started to run. We followed her, bolting wildly through the studio corridors. Three times someone tried to stop us. Each time McNally shouted, "Security!" and flashed his badge.

When we burst into the studio the Fatherly One leaped to his feet in horror. "Pleskit! What are you doing here?"

Harr-giss looked even more horrified to see us. But he quickly got his face under control, managing to make it look as if he was surprised by our breaking in, not by the fact that we had escaped from his evil plan.

He turned to the camera. "This is exactly the kind of thing I was just talking about," he said smoothly. "This alien child is totally impetuous, utterly unsuited to be in public school with our children." He reached into the pocket of his coat and pulled out a cassette. "Perhaps this is the time to show the world what I have learned," he said.

I knew it was the footage from Geembol Seven.

"That man is a traitor!" I cried.

My father looked like he was going to go into *kleptra*.

"Pleskit's telling the truth!" cried McNally. "Senator Hargis is an alien!"

The people in the studio burst out laughing. I had expected Harr-giss to be outraged, but he just laughed, as if this was too preposterous for words. I had to work hard to keep my *sphen-gnut-ksher* from flashing, since I knew if it did everyone would take it as more evidence against me.

"I can prove it!" I said. "I have brought my download box. I can download from my *sphen-gnut-ksher* the images of you threatening Tim and me."

Harr-giss looked uneasy for an instant, then slipped back into his act. "I don't know what you're talking about, son," he said. "Who the heck is Sven Not Sure anyway?"

"*Sphen-gnut-ksher*," said the Fatherly One, pronouncing it correctly and clearly working hard to stay calm, "is the name for the sensory organ on the top of our head."

"You mean that vicious weapon you carry up there?" asked Harr-giss, pointing and pretending to be terrified.

The Fatherly One scowled. "It is *not* a weapon. As everyone now knows, despite the initial misleading news reports, my son did no harm to that boy on the playground."

"He did, too!" cried a voice from the other side of the stage. "He scared the poop out of me!"

That was the first time that I realized Jordan was there. Harr-giss must have brought him along for audience sympathy.

"Fear is a great weapon all by itself," said Harr-giss smoothly. "So are lies. Even if your boy does have something he can show us, how do we know it's not faked?"

That was when Tim made his move. Leaping from behind the chair where Harr-giss was sitting, he slapped the control disk on the back of the fake senator's neck. Instantly I whipped the control pad from my pocket and began to adjust the dials.

"Take off your mask!" I ordered.

Harr-giss just sat there, while two security guards rushed over and grabbed Tim. They lifted him off the floor, and I was afraid they were going to tear him apart.

I fiddled with the dial, terrified that I wouldn't be able to make it work.

"Take off your mask!" I ordered again.

"Pleskit!" cried the Fatherly One, his voice a mixture of pleading and horror.

The men began to haul Tim away. Jordan was laughing hysterically.

And the entire world was watching.

I adjusted the dial one more time.

"Take off your mask!" I ordered.

Slowly Senator Hargis moved his hands to his neck and began to peel off his false face.

CHAPTER
25
[TIM]

The Stars

The weird thing about Harr-giss taking off his mask was that he didn't really look all that inhuman. Sure, humans don't have scaly gray skin. But he was put together pretty much the same way that we are. I think it was the shock of it that really upset people. Well, that and the way his hair stood up and started moving and hissing like hundreds of tiny snakes.

The two guards who had been about to carry me out of the studio put me down.

Jordan fainted, which was fine with me. At least it shut him up.

Meenom Ventrah stood and faced the cameras. "People of Earth! I am as shocked as you by this turn of events, and wish to apologize to you on behalf of all the ethical members of the Interplanetary Trading Federation. I guarantee you that I will work in concert with the governments of Earth to discover how this charade came to pass, and if there are any other disguised off-worlders working in positions of power."

That was when I understood that it wasn't really over. Even though we had proved Harr-giss was a fraud, the hate and suspicion he had been fanning were not his creations. He simply took advantage of what was already there. And that hate was not going to go away just because he had been unmasked. It might even get worse, because his unmasking would convince the people who believed in alien plots that they were right.

And maybe they were. Suddenly I realized it was possible there were more Harr-giss types out there, ready to undercut what Meenom was trying to do.

I'd been waiting all my life for the aliens to get here. But at the same time other people had been fearing it, or had simply believed it would never happen, or perhaps had never thought about it at all. They were the ones Meenom was speaking to now, as he looked directly into the camera.

"My friends, I understand that all this is strange and frightening. Please believe me when I say that every planet in the federation—and there are over a hundred thousand of us—has gone through the same thing. You exist for centuries, for millennia, thinking that your planet is the center of every-thing. Then, slowly, you start to understand how big the universe really is, how your own little planet is no more to the universe than a single grain of sand is to the vastness of the ocean—and you feel very alone. Alone, and small.

"And then, one day, another world makes con-tact, and it turns out you're not alone after all. It is as if you were raised in a tiny room all your life, and suddenly the walls were torn down and you found yourself facing the vastness and the strangeness of the world around you. It is excit-ing, but terrifying.

"I tell you now that the universe is even vaster and stranger than you yet imagine, and the oppor-tunities it holds even more exciting than you can guess. But it will take time to build the bridges that will connect us. I ask that you be patient with us—and I vow that I will try to be patient with you.

"There is much to be done. Let us do it to-gether, in good faith."

★　　★　　★

My mother was waiting outside the studio. When we came out, she rushed over and threw her arms around me.

"Mom!" I said, feeling embarrassed. I was even more embarrassed when I saw Linnsy standing behind her.

"Listen, buster," said my mother, "you scare me that much, you can suffer a public hug. Linnsy had come down to tell me you were going to Pleskit's house, and we saw it all on TV. I can't decide whether I should ground you for a year or give you a few hundred 'Get Out of a Goof-up Free' passes."

"Give him the passes, then ground him," said Linnsy. "They can balance each other out."

"Thanks, pal!"

Linnsy shrugged. "Any time, buddy. Just remember, if you do something like this again and don't include me, you'll wish you *were* grounded."

"Come on," I said. "Let me introduce you to Pleskit."

Meenom invited Mom and Linnsy to come back to the embassy with us so we could all have a full tour. Unfortunately, once we got there, we discovered that Mikta-makta-mookta had managed to escape. But even that could not dampen

165

our high spirits for long, since Meenom would be sending word of her crimes back to his bosses.

"As they were the ones who assigned her to me, they now owe me several pounds of apology," he said, sounding quite satisfied. "This will give me more freedom in how I make deals here on the planet—which will be good for all of us."

I had already seen most of the embassy, so for me the best thing about the tour was that it got me off the hook with Linnsy. But when Shhh-foop invited us to stay to dinner, I was the one who had to beg off.

I really didn't think my stomach could handle it.

Late that night I slipped out of our apartment. Standing in the darkness I looked at the bridge, hung with twinkling lights, that led across the river. Next I gazed at the strangely beautiful embassy, rising from the top of the hill, and thought of my new friend. Finally I turned my eyes to the vast sweep of the heavens and studied the stars, where Pleskit had come from, where I plan to go.

I stood there for the longest time, just looking.

CHAPTER
26
[PLESKIT]

A Letter Home
(Translation)

FROM: Pleskit Meenom, on Planet Earth
TO: Maktel Geebrit, on Planet Hevi-Hevi

Dear Maktel:

Well, I survived my first week of school on
Earth. It was rather more interesting than I expected. I am attaching a file that will tell you
some of the things that went on.

The best news is, I have made a friend! His
name is Tim Tompkins. He is a little *gib-stikkle*,
but I like him anyway.

I still miss Hevi-Hevi, of course, but at least I
do not feel totally alone here. I guess I'll give

up my plan to steal a spaceship and fly home.
(Just joking!)

This is a very strange place, but I think I may learn to like it after all.

I hope you can come visit sometime.

Until then—*Fremmix Bleeblom!*

Your pal,
Pleskit

About the Author and the Illustrator

BRUCE COVILLE, the author of more than sixty books for young readers, was born in Syracuse, New York. He grew up in a rural area north of the city, around the corner from his grandparents' dairy farm, where he often dreamed of traveling to other planets. His favorite writers included Hugh Lofting, Eleanor Cameron, and (a little later) Edgar Rice Burroughs.

In the years before he began to make his own living as a writer, Bruce worked as a gravedigger, a toymaker, an elementary-school teacher, and a magazine editor (among other things). Now he mostly writes, but also spends a fair amount of time traveling to speak at schools and conferences. He also produces and directs unabridged recordings of fantasy novels written for children.

Bruce and his wife, Katherine, live in an old brick house in Syracuse, which they share with a number of rather strange animals and whichever of their three children happens to be home at the moment.

Bruce's best-known books include *My Teacher Is an Alien*, *Goblins in the Castle*, and *The Skull of Truth*.

TONY SANSEVERO received his art education from Boston's Massachusetts College of Art. He has illustrated several picture books and YA novels, and is an award-winning fine artist as well. He lives in Syracuse, NY, with a menagerie of weird animals and his collection of sci-fi toys.

SPECIAL BONUS: On the next pages you will find Part One of "Disaster on Geembol Seven"— the story of what happened to Pleskit on the last planet where he lived before coming to Earth.

This story will be told in six thrilling installments included at the ends of the first six books in the *I WAS A SIXTH GRADE ALIEN* series.

Look for the next installment
at the end of Book 2:

THE ATTACK OF THE TWO-INCH TEACHER!

Coming soon . . .

**I LOST MY GRANDFATHER'S BRAIN
PEANUT BUTTER LOVER BOY**

DISASTER ON GEEMBOL SEVEN

Part One:
Night of the Moondance

FROM: Pleskit Meenom, on Planet Earth
TO: Maktel Geebrit, on Planet Hevi-Hevi

Dear Maktel:
Ever since I got in so much trouble on Geembol Seven you have been nagging me to tell you what really happened there.

I think I'm finally ready to do so.

Why?

Well, for one thing the Fatherly One is very pleased with me for my part in unmasking too-tricky Harr-Giss and his plot to ruin our mission.

So I am not quite so sensitive about this story anymore.

For another thing, I now have *two* of you tweaking my *sphen-gnut-ksher* to tell the story—you, and my new friend Tim Tompkins! I figure neither one of you is going to leave me alone until I explain what happened.

And, to tell the truth, I am sick of keeping it to myself.

Even so, I probably won't write it down all at once, because I still find it distressing.

But here is how it began:

Fourteen planets orbit the star Geembol. Of these, only two support life. And only one of these, Geembol Seven, is a member of the Interplanetary Trading Federation. (The intelligent creatures on Geembol Five are basically clouds with brains, and have nothing to trade.)

The Fatherly One was pleased when we were sent to Geembol Seven. The world is very beautiful, which makes it a choice assignment. Not only that, he was being given a promotion to full ambassador.

I was less happy, because I did not want to leave the world we were on, where I had made many friends. But that is the nature of the Fatherly One's job, of course. We will always be travelers.

Anyway, we had only been on the planet for a few days when the year's first *Moomjit* occurred. This is what they call it when all their moons—they have twelve—are full at the same time. It happens only twice a year, and when it does they have a special celebration called a moondance. Everyone goes out to look at the sky, and dance and party and carry on. People set up rides and games. There are booths with all kinds of food. They have sing-offs, and dance competitions. Everyone stays out until almost morning, even the kids.

I was out with the Fatherly One and some of his friends. The streets were filled with people—which, on Geembol Seven, means beings that look sort of like red jellyfish on stilts—and most of them were dancing in the moonlight. I got all wrapped up in watching the dancing. This was a fairly weird sight, since the people of Geembol Seven are mostly transparent. You could see their internal organs in the moonlight as they whirled around on their stiltlike legs.

Suddenly I realized I had gotten separated from

the Fatherly One. This didn't bother me at first. I knew my way back to the embassy, and Geembol Seven is considered a safe world, especially for children. And the Fatherly One had given me some money so I could buy a snack if we got separated.

I had just bought some candied waterbugs—they have the best waterbugs of anywhere on Geembol Seven, really sweet and crunchy—when I noticed this skinny green kid staring at me. It was clear that, like me, he was an offworlder. He looked kind of sad and lonely, something I could understand. So I held out the sack and asked him if he wanted a bug.

He shook his head.

Then he burst into tears.

Since he had six eyes, this made for a pretty soggy situation.

"What's the matter?" I asked.

Instead of answering, the kid turned and ran.

If I had had any sense, I would have let him go. I didn't know him. He hadn't asked for help. And I really had to go look for the Fatherly One.

I have no sense. I took off after the boy, dodging between the swaying bodies of dancing Geembolians. Strange music filled the air. The joyful odor of the dancers was so strong it made me dizzy.

The green boy ducked between someone's legs, nearly toppling him to the ground. I dodged around the dancer as he staggered, trying to keep his balance. His partner yelled at me as if it was my fault—the first angry words I had heard since we arrived on Geembol Seven.

We were headed downhill, toward the harbor. The crowd was thicker there, and I had to work hard to keep the boy in sight. I should have turned back, but I am foolishly stubborn, and once I had started the chase I did not want to give it up.

The moons sparkled on the water, and the sea beasts had risen to the surface, as if they were celebrating, too.

The green boy stopped and leaned against a building, as if to catch his breath. I sped forward, but when I was within a few paces of him, he started off again, heading down a dark alley.

I should not have followed.

I did.

The alley brought us out to a nearly empty street, one that was not part of the festival. The sounds of music and laughter were more distant now. The light of the twelve full moons made it

nearly as bright as day, though it was a cold light, and made the deserted street seem eerie, almost ghostlike.

"Wait!" I cried.

To my surprise, the boy stopped.

I hurried forward. "Why did you run?" I asked, holding my hand to my side, which hurt from the chase.

He was still weeping from all six eyes. "I am in terrible trouble."

"Well, I'm not going to hurt you."

He looked around nervously. "It's not safe here. If you want to talk, if you want to help, we have to keep going."

I should have turned back. I did not.

We continued down the streets toward the waterfront, moving eastward, away from the celebration.

In the old section of the city we came to the great docks, built hundreds of years before. The ancient wooden pilings that supported the docks were so thick, I could not reach my arms around them. We sat in front of one of them, looking out at the sea, the reflected moons, the silver-blue gabill-fish leaping joyously toward the sky.

After a moment of silence the boy said, "Why did you follow me?"

I was still trying to answer, when the piling opened behind me. A cold hand thrust forward and closed over my mouth.

Struggling, trying to scream but unable to, I was pulled into the darkness.

To be continued . . .